Romancing the Complicated Girl

A Romantic Comedy Novel

ANGIE PEPPER

Chapter 1

Tuesday

Megan Gardenia was about to ruin yet another potential romance. In record time.

The timer started when she walked into Sweet Caroline Antiques, located up the street from the flower shop where Megan and her sister worked.

Megan hadn't been looking for a date. She'd only gone in to see if they had any special vases. Sometimes Megan's flower shop customers turned their noses up at the inexpensive vases that Gardenia Flowers carried.

That was when Megan first met Duncan, the young man who introduced himself as the owner of the shop.

He didn't have any vases under a thousand dollars, but he did have a question.

"Is that Delilah's place any good?"

Megan replied, "Who wants to know?"

In her own head, Megan was funny and sassy, like a heroine in a rom-com movie. Other people—boring people—felt that Megan's approach to introductions could use some refining. Maybe she shouldn't spit on her palm before shaking hands with people. Maybe folks needed some time to warm up to her particular sense of humor.

Duncan didn't flinch.

Megan liked that about the guy. She took another look at him as a potential partner for fun and games.

Duncan had long hair. Duncan wore a goatee. Duncan was short. Those were three strikes against him, but he did have nice eyes.

"I'm the one who's asking," Duncan said casually. "Do you know the local neighborhood or not?"

He was issuing her a challenge. She liked that. This guy had some nitro in his fuel line.

"I know everything and everyone," she said. "I'm friends with Luca Lowell, the owner of Ralph's Garage."

"Am I supposed to know who that is?"

"He's kind of a big deal, Duncan. Try to keep up." She walked over to the antique store's door and checked the posted hours. "You're closed now," she said.

"I'm *trying* to close up shop, but a cute girl came in to flirt with me and waste my time asking about vases."

A tingle went up Megan's spine. She liked the attitude on this guy.

"Well, you're closed now," Megan said. "And you're hungry, because who isn't starving after a long day of not yelling at customers?" She looked him over again and nodded. "Okay. Yes."

"Yes?"

"I'll let you buy me dinner at Delilah's."

Duncan rubbed his goatee, which Megan was hating more than ever.

"That's a better offer than I ever get from my stepmom," Duncan said. "It's way better, because your offer actually includes food. I don't know what my father was thinking. Oh, wait. I think I do." He mimed cupping a pair of very large boobs.

"You're weird," she said.

"*You're* weird," he said. "But you're not my stepmom, so what the heck. Let's get drunk and see what happens."

Duncan grabbed his keys and locked up the antiques store.

They walked down Baker Street toward the cafe with the giant teapot over the door.

Megan said, "I like you, Duncan. Even though you're short, and you have a horrible, scraggly goatee."

"Uh, thanks?"

"It's not easy to meet a guy with a sense of humor. My last sorta-boyfriend always said I was emasculating him. I told him to try growing some male body parts and maybe I wouldn't. I sent him a box of tampons. He didn't think it was funny at all." She waved her hand emphatically. "No sense of humor."

"People need to relax," Duncan said. "Everyone's so sensitive about everything."

"The world has gone crazy," Megan agreed. "People need to take a joke like you, Short Duncan."

"I know I'm short," Duncan said. "So why would I care if someone told me?"

"Exactly," she said.

"We're all the same height lying down," he said.

She snorted with glee. The interaction was going well. Maybe Duncan would soon be her boyfriend.

Alas, little did Megan know that he would not.

Not this summer and not ever.

Megan Gardenia didn't know it yet, but the clock was ticking, and she was halfway to ruining her chances with Duncan from Sweet Caroline Antiques.

They arrived at Delilah's, where the waitress gave them a seat in one of the booths that was usually reserved for large parties.

Duncan pored over the menu while Megan chatted about herself without any prompting. She told Duncan about how she could relate to him being short because she wasn't perfect either. One of her eyes was higher than the other, and the tip of her nose wasn't quite straight. Her mother had experienced difficulty pushing Megan out, and it deviated her septum at birth. Megan's sister had been born by C-section, the lucky duck, so her nose was perfect. Plus, her head was perfectly round.

Duncan kept his gaze on the menu. "Sorry to hear about your dented head."

"No need to be sorry," she said. "As you may have noticed, I'm not one of those girls you have to drag answers out of."

"So I'm noticing."

"I'm all about personal growth," she said. "And getting people out of their comfort zone."

He glanced up from the menu, one eyebrow raised. "I know *I'm* feeling uncomfortable."

"Good. This is exactly why I go to my self-help group. To shake things up. People need to take more risks in life. My heart just aches for people who won't take a risk."

"It does?"

"One of the old dudes in my group told me last week that my honesty has helped him a lot. He gave me a big hug with his wrinkly old arms."

"Hot." Duncan smirked. "Next time, get it on video for me to watch."

The waitress came back, and Duncan ordered a pizza with onions and roasted garlic.

"Onions *and* garlic," Megan said. "So much for our make out session later."

The waitress, an older woman named Maggie who'd been working there for about a million years, sighed and gave Megan a head shake.

Megan frowned at the waitress. "What? You're not my mom."

"But I do have your mother's email address," the waitress said. "I'm not afraid to send her a full report, Meenie." The waitress had known the Gardenia sisters since they were little, and she knew their nicknames.

Megan handed the waitress her menu. "I'll have a sausage and cheese pizza." She looked right at Duncan. "I like sausage."

He winced and pulled his head back.

After the waitress left, Duncan asked, "Does this routine of yours work with the ladies you usually date?"

"Ha ha," she said. "I don't date chicks."

"Their loss," he said. "Is your name really Megan?"

"Yup."

"Then what was the name the waitress called you?"

"Meenie. M-E-E-N-I-E. My sister's name is Tina, so we're Teenie and Meenie. It's a rhyming thing, not because I'm mean."

"Right." He slow-blinked. "Who would *ever* say you were mean? You've already told me I'm short, and you don't like my goatee, and you keep frowning at my hair. Who would say that's mean? That's what nice girls do."

"Honesty is caring," she said.

"Is it? Really?"

She looked down at the table, avoiding his eyes. "Sometimes people say I'm mean. But that's just because they're insecure and can't take a joke."

"Because most people are too sensitive," Duncan said, playing along. "They're not fun, refreshingly honest people like us."

"That's right. You get it, Short Duncan."

He picked up his import beer and took a long drink straight from the bottle.

"Light beer," Megan said, lifting her chin. "That should have been my first clue you were the sensitive type. Plus, you sell old-lady furniture for a living. I should have known. It's all making sense now. I know what your issue is."

He smiled. "Go on. Enlighten me."

"You're gay, Duncan. But that's okay. This date isn't a total bust. I might be in the market for a new gay best friend."

"I'm not gay."

"Oh, right." She snorted. "Then I guess all your lame jokes about your stepmom lusting after your body aren't overcompensation."

He took another drink.

"And you're an alcoholic," Megan said. "Half that bottle's gone already."

He shrugged. "Just trying to find the right level of alcohol that makes you more appealing." He licked his lips and squinted. "Not there yet."

Megan felt the insult register that time. Her old fighting instinct flared up instantly. Megan didn't walk away from a challenge.

"Good luck with that," she said. "I'm already at maximum appeal right now. If you can't see that, you need to get your eyes checked."

"I have bad eyes." He checked an imaginary box in the air between them. "Another flaw to add to my list of shortcomings."

"Since you're making a list, here's another thing: Your shirt is stupid. Is that supposed to be a retro bowling shirt?"

"Yeah," he said. "What's wrong with bowling shirts?"

"Uh, the nineties called, and they want their shirt back, Duncan."

He leaned back in the booth. "What's the name of that self-help group you go to? I'd like to send them a cash donation for the fantastic work they're doing."

Megan leaned back as well. She'd had enough of Duncan, who wasn't nearly as funny as he thought he was.

She slid sideways out of the booth and stood. "Have fun eating two pizzas and paying for both of them, dude. I'm out of here."

He tilted his head. "Lost your appetite?"

"Staring at a human barf bag isn't good for my appetite."

He laughed. "I'm a human barf bag? What are we, twelve?"

And that was the precise moment when the date hit rock bottom.

Megan gave Duncan the middle finger with both hands.

He gave it right back.

Megan considered tackling him and twisting back his offending fingers, but she somehow managed to turn herself around, start walking, and leave the cafe before things got worse and she got kicked out of Delilah's. Again.

When she reached the sidewalk outside, she pumped her fist.

Victory!

She was really making progress with her goal of living her best life.

Never mind the failed dinner date with Short Duncan. Things were still going well, in general.

Megan Gardenia was *really* getting in touch with her true, authentic self.

Too bad Short Duncan was too much of a sensitive snowflake to appreciate her and all her charms.

Anyway, that was what *Megan* thought about Megan.

It was pretty clear to *everyone else* that Megan was a dumpster fire with a grease fire on top.

Why *was* she like that?

There was a perfectly good explanation for why Megan was the way she was. One that would be obvious in hindsight but only once her eyes had been opened by the wise words coming from an unexpected source.

And when would she open her eyes?

Not for a while.

Not until after she'd hit a lower point than her date with Duncan.

With Megan Gardenia, life lessons had to be learned the hard way.

Chapter 2

Megan arrived home and went to lavish attention on the one guy she could always count on.

He was orange and furry. He returned her affection with an earlobe nip.

"Muffins, I thought you loved me, but you just want tuna, don't you?"

He purred louder and nipped her ear again, harder this time.

She fed him and sprinkled his supplements on top the way he liked it.

She pulled a store-bought pizza from the freezer and threw it in the microwave. Using the microwave was the worst possible way to reheat a pizza, but she was starving, and she had her self-help group that night.

As she ate the soggy-bottomed pizza, she thought about Duncan, and how he'd been fortunate enough to get two pizzas that were crisp and perfect.

Short Duncan can have his pizzas, she thought. Megan would rather be around a guy who appreciated her.

She picked up Muffins and snuggled him. "You love me," she said into his fur.

He started licking the cheese off the edge of her plate.

"My mistake," she said. "You only love cheese."

The orange cat continued stealing her food, unperturbed.

An unpleasant thought came to Megan's mind. It was a torturous, unhelpful thought in a nasty voice. At the group, they called them *intrusive thoughts*.

The intrusive thought said, *Meenie, no man can ever love you for you.*

She tried to shut it out, but that only made the intrusive voice louder. The only thing a person could do with intrusive thoughts was to introduce better ones or get moving, physically. There was also the option of a full lobotomy, but Megan wasn't there yet.

She left the pizza cheese on the floor for Muffins, shotgunned a Diet Coke, and walked out to her car, belching the whole way.

Who wouldn't love a girl like that?

She let out a couple more burps as she pulled the car into the parking lot for the community center. She parked her mother's big Cadillac at the far end, where it wouldn't get dinged any more than it already was.

Megan loved the car and the power it had. People got out of the way for a big car like that, especially one with a few dents.

She was late for the group session, but she was carrying a pan of cinnamon buns from the day before, so it would be okay. The whole group loved her baking. She could probably murder one of them at random, and the others would help her bury the body if she provided enough cinnamon buns.

Megan walked down the hallway, past the community bulletin board, and arrived at the door to Room 3C. Most groups would put a big, legible sign on the door, but their leader only taped a small business card there.

The door to Room 3C opened with a squeak. The group's leader, a beautiful blonde therapist named Feather, waved Megan in.

"Cinnamon buns," Megan announced as she put the cinnamon buns on the back table.

The person who'd been talking when Megan had interrupted, a retired librarian, started her story over with the therapist's encouragement. The librarian shared the news that things were going well with the widower she was dating.

The woman, whose name Megan could never remember, was an emotional basket case. She started crying tears of happiness. Megan looked away, scanning the other people seated on chairs in a circle, until she came to a full stop on a new face.

Whoa now! There was a new person in the circle, and it wasn't a boring white-haired person like most of them. It was a guy, and he looked about Megan's age.

The guy had dark hair—a full head of it, unlike most of the guys who showed up for help at eight o'clock on Tuesdays. He had dark eyes and refined features. He was wearing a business suit, with a tie and everything. He looked strong and intelligent. He was, to Megan, the human equivalent of a thoroughbred who'd been produced through selective breeding. He was perfect. He was a pretty, pretty pony.

The librarian's monologue about finding love in her golden years receded to a mwah-mwah-mwah of background noise as Megan focused only on the new guy, Pretty Pony.

When the turn to speak came around to him, Pretty Pony asked the group's coach, "How does this whole thing work? How many sessions does it take for people to fix their problems? Five or six?"

There was a collective gasp from the whole group.

Megan exclaimed, "Hah!"

Feather, the therapist leading the group, tucked her pale, perfectly straight hair behind her ear and licked her lips.

Megan's heart got all fluttery with excitement. Feather always licked her lips before she ripped someone a new one for a dumb question. As Feather prepared to hit Pretty Pony with both barrels, her feathered earrings swung gently. People always gave her feather-themed stuff. It was dumb, but Megan was secretly envious.

The librarian murmured to the bald man beside her, "I've lost track of how many sessions I've been for."

Feather said, "That's a good question, Andrew. As for the number—"

"Drew," he said, cutting her off. He quickly turned on a grin to soften the rudeness. "Everyone calls me Drew. I have a brother named Alan, and my mother regrets giving us both A names. Call me Drew. You were saying?"

"Drew," Feather said. "I'd love to tell you how many sessions it takes before a person solves their problems, but first, you tell me: How many ties should a man own?"

He blinked and pulled his head back, seemingly caught off guard by Feather's question. His grin dropped then came back with a vengeance, with a dimple. A dimple! Drew was a Pretty Pony with a pretty dimple.

"A man should have as many ties as he likes," Drew said. He patted his own tie, a simple blue pinstripe.

"Exactly," Feather said.

He looked down at his tie. "I don't even like this tie," he said. "It makes me look like a banker. Or worse. A politician."

The whole group laughed.

Drew said, "I don't look like someone who makes people cry for a living."

The group howled with laughter.

Megan had never heard so much laughter in that room, and she'd ripped some A-quality jokes during sessions—always to lighten the mood. People never laughed like that for her, but why would they? Megan wasn't an attractive man in a quality suit. Those guys got everything handed to them, or so people said. Obviously this guy didn't think he'd gotten enough, or he wouldn't have been there.

"Drew, forget the tie," Feather said. "It was just a metaphor. If you need help with your style, I can set you up with a colleague for some one-on-one personal shopping. I got my start as a life and style coach, and I still have a lot of contacts. Now, why don't you share a few words about why you're here?"

"A few words?" He frowned. "I don't know. My problems aren't that big. Nothing's coming to mind. Maybe I'll wait until next week."

Feather made a note in her notebook. She turned to the person seated next to Drew, a white-haired lady who'd been part of the group long before Megan started.

Feather said, "Let's hear from you, Abbie. Have you been making progress talking to your sister about your mother's reluctance to move into a more appropriate facility?"

With the dramatic sigh of someone who'd been waiting to speak, Abbie started in on the family drama.

Megan thought of it as drama, anyway. Feather didn't approve of the word *drama* because it implied that some people's problems weren't real.

Megan was so bored with Abbie and her drama. How was it that Abbie could talk to the group for ten, fifteen, twenty minutes about her sister's shortcomings but couldn't say a peep to the woman face-to-face? It was hard for Megan to relate to someone who was so weak, so simpering. Megan wondered if the real reason Abbie never confronted her sister was because she'd have to stop coming to the group and get the attention of everyone there. What a drama queen.

Megan looked over to see how the new guy was enjoying the group so far. He was paying attention to Abbie, nodding along empathetically. Either he was good at mirroring body language, or he was genuinely interested in the woman's ramblings. He slowly reached up, loosened his tie, and pulled it away.

Megan's mouth felt gummy, and her whole body was hot. Was she sweating? Talk about an overreaction. The guy had removed his tie. That was all. He hadn't exactly done a striptease.

What was his magic? Was it that he was paying attention to a woman talking about her problems and undressing at the same time? Megan's heart pounded. She'd just discovered the equivalent of pornography for women, and it was this.

Drew shrugged his way out of his suit jacket and folded it over the back of his chair, not once taking his eyes off Abbie.

Seeing this gave Megan a strange feeling. She liked Drew. She wanted to kiss him but not just that. She wanted to rub her chin on his ears. She wanted to lick his face. Megan's style of intimacy was unique, like the rest of her.

For the next hour, Megan did her best to keep her face pointed at whoever was speaking. Her eyes, however, kept darting over to explore every visible part of Drew.

Suddenly, it was her turn to talk. With all her fantasies about licking Drew's face to see if it was salty, she'd completely forgotten the talking would come around to her. All eyes were on Megan, including Drew's.

Feather asked, "Anything new with you?"

"I went on a date today," Megan said. "It was my first date with a guy I just met."

There were some murmurs of surprise from the group and one giggle.

One of the bald guys muttered something about truth being stranger than fiction.

Feather waved a hand to shush the group and prompted Megan to keep sharing. "And how did that go?"

Megan held out both hands. "You tell me. I'm down here at the community center with you losers right now. As you can see, I'm not picking my clothes off the ceiling fan at some guy's place."

A few people laughed. Not like they'd laughed for Drew with his tie comment, but it felt good.

Feather said, "What have we discussed about not calling the group *losers*?"

"Hey, I'm part of the group," Megan said. "I'm calling myself a loser too."

The librarian said, "You don't speak for all of us."

Abbie said, "My intrusive thoughts tell me I'm a loser. Maybe she's right, and we should take back the word."

One of the bald men said, "I came to this group to stop feeling like a loser."

Feather waved her hands for everyone to settle. They didn't. They continued arguing over the word *loser*.

Then Drew cleared his throat, and everyone went silent.

Drew fixed his refined brown eyes on Megan and said, "I think we'd all like to hear what went wrong on this lovely young woman's date. Or is it just me? I know I'm curious." He looked at Feather. "Is it respectful to be curious? I enjoy hearing people speak. In my line of work, they don't get much chance to talk for long stretches."

"Go ahead," Feather said to Megan. "Let's all try to be honest and curious in a respectful way. Let's show how it's done. This is Drew's introductory session, and we have had a lot of sightseers lately." She explained to Drew, "Those are people who come once and never come back. We'd like to show you an accurate representation of the work we do so you'll come back next week."

Drew grinned and pointed at Megan. "Does that mean she's auditioning for me?"

"Yeehaw," Megan said, clapping her hands. "Put me in, coach," she said to Feather.

Feather's cheeks flushed as she lost her usual composure for a moment. "I wouldn't put it that way, Drew. We're just a support group, not a reality TV show." She frowned at Megan. "Maybe we should skip you this week. I know Ryan's been working on his fear of grocery store checkouts."

"No way," Megan said. "I've been coming here a lot longer than Ryan. Besides, all of Ryan's problems are in his head."

Ryan twitched at the mention of his name and readjusted the scarf he always wore.

Feather said tiredly, "Inside our heads is where most of our problems are." She looked weary. "Otherwise talking about our problems wouldn't help."

Abbie said, "Go ahead, dear. We all want to know what happened on your date."

Megan said, "My date crashed and burned because the guy was a loser. It wasn't a problem that was in my head. He ordered a beer, and then he said he was going to drink beer until I got better looking."

Abbie gasped in horror, as did a few of the ladies. The bald guys chuckled.

Feather said, in a parental tone of warning, "Now, now. This only works if you're completely honest."

"I'm not messing around," Megan said. "That's literally what he told me."

Drew jumped in like a hero. "Young lady, if your date said that to you, then the guy must be blind or an idiot or both."

"Thank you!" Megan threw out both hands in exasperated triumph. "Thank you," she said again. "Was that so hard to say, Drew?"

His dark eyes twinkled. "It's not so hard to tell the truth," he said.

"You came to the right place for that," Megan said. "We air a bit of truth, in between the mwah-mwah-mwah."

Feather waved her hand. "That's enough cross talk."

"You need to come back every week," Megan said, ignoring the group's leader and pointing her finger at the newcomer. "We need someone around here with enough man parts to say what needs to be said." She eyed the group's coach. "No offense, Feather."

Feather made a tsk sound then turned her body to a new angle and gently said, "Ryan, are you ready to share next? Did you read that article I sent you about polyvagal theory?"

"I'm not sure I understand the breathing," Ryan said, fidgeting with his scarf. "My diaphragm doesn't do what I want."

"It takes time," Feather said. "And patience. You can't expect to turn around a lifetime of developing neural pathways in a few weeks."

Drew quipped, "Because it takes eight sessions, right?"

Everyone laughed at Drew's joke, including Ryan.

Feather said to Ryan, "You just laughed. Did you notice that? It means you're in a relaxed state right now. Can you tell us how that feels inside your body?"

Ryan put his hand on his belly and started fumbling around for the words. "Light? No. Breezy?"

Megan's brain tuned him out and everything else on the audio spectrum.

She didn't need sound when she had visuals. Ryan's crippling fear of the revolving belts at grocery store checkouts would still be around in all its weird glory next week and the week after that.

All Megan cared about was staring at Drew, the hot new guy in the fancy suit who made everyone laugh.

As soon as the formal part of the group session ended, Megan was going to make even more of an impression on the new guy, with more than just her cinnamon buns.

Chapter 3

After everyone had shared and aired their issues, Feather gave a few words of general advice, something about being perfect so people could love you. It was easy for her to say since she was already perfect. Then she dismissed them.

Everyone headed toward the back table for refreshments. There were only twelve members present, but they sounded like three times as many as they stampeded toward the coffee and sweets.

The thermos of coffee was half-decaffeinated—or half-caffeinated, for the optimists. Its aroma quickly filled the air.

Megan's cinnamon buns were an instant hit. As usual, people joked about calling the group Carbohydrate Lovers Anonymous.

Abbie wielded a shining spatula, her big grin taking ten years off her face. "I'm Abbie, and I'm a Carboholic!"

Ryan flung the end of his scarf over his shoulder dramatically and declared, "I'm Ryan, and I'm also a Carboholic."

The retired librarian turned to Megan and said, "Oh, Meenie, you spoil us so good. It's treats like these that make us keep you around."

"Ha ha," Megan said. "This group would fall asleep if it wasn't for me, and you know it."

The others said nothing.

Drew, who'd been pouring a half-caff, paused mid-pour. He said to the retired librarian, "Excuse me, but did you just call this lovely girl a *meanie*?"

"That's who she is," the librarian said.

"You have to spell it for him," Abbie said to the librarian while excavating a cinnamon bun for herself.

The librarian explained to Drew, "We call her Meenie with two E's, M-E-E-N-I-E. It's short for something." She blinked at Megan. "Sorry, love. I don't remember if that's your real name or a nickname. Is it ethnic?" She turned and scanned the group.

Abbie said, "She doesn't look ethnic to me, but I don't see color. I adore everyone equally. Unlike my horrible sister, who has a problem with the kinds of ethnic people who work at the seniors' facility."

Feather interrupted to say, "We don't talk about our big issues during the coffee chat. This time is supposed to be for pleasantries only."

Everyone went silent.

Feather pulled out her phone and left the area.

Megan walked over to Drew and said, "You heard the woman. Make pleasantries with me."

"Or what?" His dark eyes were playful. "Will I get in trouble?"

"Yes but not with me. Feather will kick your butt."

"It seems like she runs a tight ship."

"She's kind of rigid, but underneath the feather earrings is a great coach. You made the right choice coming here, dude. She'll definitely help you with your issues. What were you saying they were, exactly?"

He gave her a knowing look. "This time is for pleasantries only. You're a mean girl, *Meenie*. You're trying to get me in trouble."

She rolled her eyes. "I know you're not here for booze or gambling because there are dedicated groups for those down the hall."

"Then I must be here for something else," he said.

"You must be."

"Maybe I came here to make an investment in *myself*."

He brought the cup of watered-down coffee to his lips and took a sip. That gave Megan a view of his lips in action, which gave her a funny, warm feeling.

Around them, everyone else was making pleasantries. Mostly they were joking about being Carboholics.

Megan stood on her toes to look at the top of Drew's head. He had lush, dark-brown hair. Unlike Duncan, there was nothing short about him, nothing lacking at all, from what she could see. His hair was cut in a conservative style, and he didn't have any facial hair. He was well over six feet tall, and he didn't smell of cologne, but he did smell of something that was clean and refreshing.

He said, "Can I get you anything?"

"Juice," she said. "That's what I need."

"Is that all you need?"

Grinning at how well things were going, she turned away to grab a bottle of orange juice from the table. When she turned back around, Drew was so close, he was practically on top of her.

He was doing something odd. He had his elbows flared out at his sides, which made him wide, like a wall. Megan, who usually stepped forward in response to a challenge, surprised herself by stepping back. He took a step forward, tentatively. She took a step back. They were dancing, sort of. He grinned and kept moving forward, enjoying the game, tacking from side to side as she kept her distance.

She asked, "What are you doing, dude? Are you herding me? Like some sort of sheep herding dog?"

He said only, "Woof."

She kept backing up, playing along. "Oh, so I'm a helpless little lamb, is that it?"

"Woof," he replied, softly enough that the others making pleasantries wouldn't hear.

"I'm not a lamb or a sheep," Megan said. "I'm the opposite of a sheep. I cannot be herded. I am unherdable."

Despite her claim to be unherdable, Megan continued to allow herself to be separated from the herd.

Drew didn't stop until they reached the big window overlooking the courtyard. The sun had set, and the shrubs and garden were lit by strings of white fairy lights. It was a nice view and a pleasant place to be herded to.

Megan stopped with her back to the window. "There's nowhere left to go except on top of me," she said.

He said, "How long do pleasantries usually last?"

She cleared her throat and tried to look coy. "Don't tell me you're one of those guys who goes to self-help groups to pick up chicks with low self-esteem. I bet you watch that movie *Fight Club* over and over."

"Never seen it," he said.

"Great film," she said and proceeded to give him a full but fast synopsis, spoiling the twist ending immediately.

"You just saved me two hours," he said, which wasn't what most people would have said.

"You're welcome," she said. "How do you like your first group therapy session?"

He glanced around. "I like the pleasantries." He sipped his coffee again, wincing at the taste. "What is this, chicory? It's so bad."

"Isn't coffee supposed to taste bad? My sister says all coffee tastes like a goat's backside, even the good stuff."

He glanced over at the flock then back at Megan. "You have a sister? What's she like?"

"I love my sister. She's also my best friend." Tina always claimed that Rory was her best friend, but Megan figured it was only to boost Rory's self-esteem. Who would pick Rory over Megan?

Megan unscrewed the cap from her orange juice bottle and raised it to her mouth.

Drew said, "If your sister's half as pretty as you, she must be a supermodel."

Megan choked on the unexpected compliment. The orange juice in her mouth had nowhere to go, except all over Drew's face and his crisp dress shirt.

He didn't back away or flinch. He took it with the practiced ease of someone who had been sprayed plenty.

He stuck out his tongue and licked the beads of orange juice off his lips.

"The juice was a much better choice than the coffee," he said.

"That juice was in my mouth."

"Should I be worried? Where else has your mouth been?"

"The usual places."

"I'm not afraid of a little saliva," Drew said.

A warm sensation crept up Megan's body. Her face felt itchy and hot. Was she blushing? Megan never blushed. Why did her cheeks feel like they were on fire? Was she coming down with something?

With her gaze fixed on his, she brought the orange juice back up to her lips and took another drink. A big one. She shotgunned the whole bottle while he watched.

When she was done, he asked, "Mouth clear? Permission to speak?"

"All out of ammunition." She opened her mouth and stuck out her tongue.

Then he did another odd thing. He ducked his head and peered into her mouth, as though inspecting it. He didn't do it for long, but Megan noticed.

She asked, "See anything you like in my face orifice?"

He smirked. "Your face orifice looks healthy to me."

"I'm glad I passed your inspection, Mr. Sheep Herder. What's next?"

"You tell me," he said. His eyes said it was time for a move to be made.

Megan cut him off at the pass. "I'm not going to hook up with you," she said.

"What?" He was confused, or at least feigning confusion.

"A few months ago, sure. I would have trotted right out of here with any cute guy who showed interest. But what I've learned is that guys like you, guys who *look like you*, aren't worth it."

"We're not?"

"Guys like you are terrible at sex. Just terrible."

He continued to have, or feign, confusion. "Why would you say that?"

"You're too attractive," she said. "With your face and your hair and your nice suit. You didn't learn how to be a good lover because you don't stick around long enough to get practice."

He tugged at his collar. "That's not fair to say."

"I'm not some sheltered girl who doesn't know about the world," she said. "Pretty boys like you make a sport out of sleeping with as many girls as they can. You're all about the quantity, not the quality." She pointed at him. "And that's why you're here tonight. You need help with your sex addiction."

"That's not why I'm here."

"It's not? Then tell me why you're here."

He glanced over at the group and then at Feather. All of them were well out of earshot and wouldn't have known.

"We're not supposed to talk about that stuff now," he said. "Can't we go back to making pleasantries?"

"Sure we can, Drew. But you need to know something if things are going to move forward with us. I'm not the simple, straightforward nice girl I seem to be."

He suppressed a smile. "You're not?"

"I'm… complicated," she said.

He nodded and took a step back. "Maybe complicated is what I need. In my day job, I'm the one giving all the orders. It's a lot of responsibility, and it's lonely. Nobody ever stands up to me or calls me out on anything."

"Is that why you're here? Everyone at work respects you too much?" Megan laughed hollowly. "Dude, you'd better come up with something juicier than that because you are *not* going to get a lot of airtime with this group."

Very plainly, he said, "If I knew what my problem was, I'd tell you."

"So you're here for a problem, but you don't know what it is?"

"Is that so hard to believe?"

"How do you know you have a problem if you don't know what it is?"

"Well, what are you here for?"

"Isn't it obvious? There's no problem. I'm only here to support the other people. I don't need therapy because I'm already awesome."

"You *are* awesome," he said. "And fearsome."

"I'd be mad at you if I was a hundred percent sure you just insulted me."

"I'd like to see you get mad at me."

She gave him another look from head to toe. "Drew, something tells me there's more to you than your pretty face and nice suit."

He looked down at his orange juice–soaked dress shirt. "I should get home and put some prewash on this before it sets."

"Yeah, you should." Megan nodded and pretended she knew what prewash was.

He started to turn away but paused. "Are you coming to the session next Tuesday?"

"Maybe."

"I hope you do," he said, sounding utterly sincere, and he walked back over to the group.

Chapter 4

Wednesday

Megan Gardenia was confident she could have woken up Wednesday morning next to Drew, if she'd wanted to.

Instead, she woke up to sweet little kisses coming from her most loyal man. Muffins was on her chest, licking her chin and rubbing his wet nose on her face.

When she opened her eyes, Muffins gave her a surprised look, as though he was *shocked* she wouldn't sleep right through the application of his raspy tongue on her face.

"Good morning, Prince Charming," she said.

Muffins pulled his face back, displeased by the morning breath of his mistress. He retreated to the foot of the bed and stretched out his pleasantly plump orange body. Megan's sea-foam-green bedding was a perfect complement to his fur, which was why she'd chosen that color. As disagreeable as Megan could be, she loved the harmony of complementary colors.

Cat and mistress got up, got breakfast, and sat by the window that looked out at the backyard. Megan's sister Tina—the Teenie to Megan's Meenie nickname—lived back there, in the former garage that their mother, Lois Gardenia, had converted into a cottage. Lois had intended to rent the place out—she was a savvy businesswoman—but Tina had parked herself in there, and Tina always got what she wanted. Their mother favored Tina. It must have been Tina's straight nose and perfectly round head.

Megan crunched her toast and stared at the windows of the cottage. The blinds were closed, which meant Tina was being paranoid about being seen by Megan, or she had Luca over.

Tina and Luca had met back during prom season, at a time of year when Tina normally would be spiraling into depression. It was nearly fall now, and the two were going strong.

Megan was happy for Tina and Luca but also envious. It was hard not to be envious of the gorgeous, pretty Tina Gardenia, who could have easily been a supermodel if she'd grown an extra quarter inch. The girls were close in age, only eleven months apart. Lois had still been nursing Tina when she got pregnant with Megan by accident.

When it was time for Megan to emerge from the womb, she barged her way to the exit, not waiting for the planned C-section. Out she came, the traditional way, with her pointy head and tilted nose, about half as cute as Tina had been as a newborn.

In school, Megan was nearly as smart as Tina in every subject but not quite. Every teacher compared Megan to her sister, who'd been their pupil the previous year. Every time, Megan fell short.

Megan's only opportunity to stand on her own would have to come by doing something her sister wasn't interested in. One night, in front of Lois and Tina, Megan announced she was joining the girls' wrestling team at the high school. Tina, who'd been thinking about joining the drama club to get closer to a guy named Jonathan, declared, for the first time ever, that she'd always been interested in wrestling, and she might join the team as well. Within seconds, the girls had the coffee table pushed aside and were tangling with each other on the area rug, both laughing like maniacs in front of their horrified mother.

Once they'd finished the match, Lois said to her daughters, "Teenie, wouldn't it be nice to let Meenie have something just to herself?"

Tina took her eyes off Megan, who took the opportunity to body-slam her sister, crushing her perfect nose into the floral rug. It felt good.

"It's okay, Mom," Megan said as she held her sister down. "Teenie can join wrestling with me. I don't mind."

Lois said, "I completely understand your desire to kick your older sister's butt, and you can do so, but only if there is adult supervision at all the matches and practices."

"There will be," Megan said.

Tina said something that was muffled by the rug.

Practice started the next day at school. The kids were supervised by adults, for the most part. What their mother didn't know, and couldn't have predicted, was how much trouble the Gardenia sisters would get into on trips to other towns for matches.

Tina started dating Jonathan not long after the girls joined the wrestling team, so she was off the dating market, but Megan got her pick of all the other guys at wrestling events. And there were always a lot of guys. Fit, active, healthy, energetic guys.

Megan had a lot of fun with guys over the years—wrestling and other activities—but she was approaching the ripe old age of thirty. She'd noticed that the guys her age were changing.

When she'd been younger, guys were interested in girls, period. Any kind. But now, guys her age were more choosey. They seemed to separate girls into two kinds: the marrying kind and the okay-for-now kind.

Megan feared she might never become the marrying kind. Her sister would get married to Luca Lowell, and it would probably happen soon. Unfortunately for Megan, Luca didn't have any brothers, and Tina wouldn't share Luca with

Megan—Megan had asked a few times, joking—well, mostly joking.

What was Megan going to do after all her friends and the guys her age were married off? Who would she hang out with?

She'd have to continue dating guys who were into girls of any type. Guys who were no older than twenty-seven. Guys who laughed when she shotgunned a Diet Coke and belched the national anthem then did the same.

But was that even something she wanted? Wouldn't that get boring? How many times could you belch a song before it lost the wow factor?

Last night at the group meeting, she'd been surprised by how attracted she'd been to the new guy, Drew.

She wondered what Drew was doing that day at his job where people respected him too much—*boohoo*.

She reached into her pocket and pulled out a card. It was the business card she'd taken from Short Duncan's antique shop. She'd picked it up before he'd shown her their overpriced vases and before he'd ruined his chances to date her by being so rude at Delilah's.

Short Duncan was clearly not a very good judge of character, but on the positive side, he wasn't afraid to tell Megan what he thought.

That gave her an idea. What if Duncan could reveal some secrets about what guys his age wanted in a date?

It wouldn't hurt for Megan to get a few tips. She hadn't become an excellent wrestler without some help from the coaches.

She figured Duncan would probably limit his comments to easy, fixable things like wardrobe choices and hair. Did guys even care about clothes and hair? Was that all that separated the okay-for-now girl from the marrying kid? She'd have to find out.

Megan would need to work at the flower shop in the afternoon, but she had her morning free.

She cleaned up from breakfast and headed straight over to Sweet Caroline Antiques for some dating tips.

Chapter 5

Duncan was talking to another man when Megan walked into Sweet Caroline Antiques.

Duncan gave her a polite nod, not acknowledging that she was anything more to him than a potential customer.

Megan walked over to a cabinet full of teacups and pretended to be interested in a fancy tea set while listening in.

Duncan and the man, who seemed to be a private investigator, talked for a few minutes, then the man left.

Megan came over to the glass counter, leaned on it, and asked, "Why were you and that dude talking about locating some chick? Are you stalking someone?"

"You wish." Duncan puffed out his chest and ran his hand through his long sandy-brown hair. He was cuter than she remembered, like someone who should have been on a surfboard, not standing behind the counter of a dusty antiques store.

"Dude, I heard you talking," she said. "Who are you looking for? Maybe I can help."

"It's not a big deal," he said. "My friend lost track of someone, and I think it was a mistake."

"A *girl* someone. Hey, was that guy's name Cooper? He's an actual private investigator, isn't he? I think I know about that guy."

Duncan didn't say anything.

Megan realized what was different about him that day. "Your goatee," she said. "You shaved it off. Good for you."

Duncan rubbed his smooth chin. "I've been meaning to shave it off anyway. I didn't do it because of you. I should have done it before summer because now my chin is lighter than the rest of my face."

"You look fine," she said. "You actually look really good."

He grinned.

"But you're still short," she said.

"Not where it counts," he said.

"Keep it family friendly, dude. I'm only here as a friend, not your concubine."

"We're friends now? I'd hate to see how you treat your enemies."

"Ha ha," she said. "Don't you want to be friends?"

"I'm still not gay," he said.

"I won't hold it against you."

Duncan shrugged. "Fine. We're friends. What can I do for you, friend?"

"I need you to tell me what's wrong with me."

He blinked. "Nope." He backed away and grabbed a broom and dustpan. "Not around all these priceless and very breakable antiques. No way."

"You don't have to be mean," she said. "Just give me a few pointers that I can work on. I want to be the kind of girl that guys buy jewelry for. And motorbikes."

"Why don't you buy your own motorbike?"

"That's not the point."

He started sweeping the floor, not meeting her gaze. Without looking up, he said, "I got your pizza packed up last night. It's in the fridge here if you want it."

"Really? That sausage pizza would make a tasty lunch. What do I owe you?"

He leaned the broom against the counter and excused himself to a back room. He returned with a pizza box.

She opened it. There was a slice missing.

He named his price. She negotiated him down to half and gave him the cash.

"You're not as bad as I thought," she said, taking a bite from the tip of a cold slice.

"I'll take that as a compliment." He handed her a napkin.

"What about me? What are my top redeeming qualities, would you say?"

He picked up a ceramic figurine from the counter between them and gently tucked it into a cupboard.

"You've got a lot going for you," he said.

"Such as?"

"It's hard to put my finger on."

"It's nothing, right? That's mean, dude."

"No, I'm getting to it. You've got something. Here's the thing: I go to auctions all the time. And I always get the deals. The key is being able to spot value, being able to tell trash from the real deal."

"Are you calling me trash?"

"No," he said. "You just *appear to be* trash at first glance."

She was too stunned to speak. She shoved the pizza in her mouth.

"But it's just the appearance of trash on the surface," Duncan said. "Underneath is a treasure. You're like an old sideboard that's been painted over."

She swallowed the pizza. "I'm like an old sideboard that's been painted over?"

"With a bad color, like purple." He took a few steps away and patted a wooden piece of furniture that had been restored to its original wood finish. "Like this sideboard."

"I'm trash? Purple trash?"

"Yes but not all the way down. There's something good underneath this." He waved at her in general. "Underneath this whole tough-girl act you put on."

Megan had been starting to feel bad—being called trash could have that effect on a person—but suddenly, a thought occurred to her. Duncan was running a game on her. A game! It was so obvious.

Duncan asked, "Why are you smiling like that? You're not going to smash things, are you?"

"You're doing that thing," she said, pointing at him. "The pickup artists do it. You give a girl negative attention, so she'll feel bad about herself, and then she'll beg you to sleep with her."

"I'm not doing that," he said. "Why? Is it working?"

She kept jabbing her finger at him. "You are one sick puppy, dude. I came over here for honesty and friendship, and you tried to take advantage of me."

"I answered your question," he said. "You can't be mad at me for giving you what you wanted."

She grabbed the pizza box and stepped toward the door. "Thanks for nothing, Short Duncan. You should grow your goatee back. You've got a weak chin, and it's lighter than the rest of your dumb face." She turned and headed for the door.

"Thank you for stopping in," he called after her. "I'll see you around."

"Not if I see you first!"

Chapter 6

Six Days Later

Tuesday

Megan was the first to arrive at room 3C, so she started arranging the chairs in the usual circle.

Feather came in next, floating on a cloud of bliss for whatever reason. Probably because she was so deliriously happy about being perfect and amazing that she was high on her own fumes.

Megan was not in a great mood.

Feather looked over the tiny square cakes Megan was arranging on the snack table. "Those look adorable," she said. "How are you doing, Meenie?"

"I dunno. The tea cakes turned out all right. You can have one now, if you don't want to wait until everyone else has pawed them over."

Feather tucked her perfect, platinum-blond hair behind one ear. "Meenie, the last time I saw you bring something so elaborate, your grandmother had just passed away. Is there anything you'd like to talk about before the others get here?"

"Maybe. Do you think a person's name can change how a person is?"

"Are you talking about your name? I can call you Megan, if you'd prefer."

"No need. I'm just curious. That's all. Like in an abstract way."

"It's good to be curious. That's an important part of self-growth."

"It's funny too," Megan said. "Your name is Feather, and you look like a feather. You're dainty and wispy. You're soft and soothing to people, but you still have that core of strength."

"Thank you," Feather said. "That's a very kind thing for you to say."

"I can be nice. People don't think I'm nice, but I am. Honestly."

"I know you are. I've seen you help people in the group. And you help me too. People would probably fall asleep if you weren't here."

"They would," Megan agreed.

Feather took one of the tiny cakes and ate it delicately.

Megan said, "Back to your name, though. Do you think you'd be a totally different person if your name was something regular, like…" Megan couldn't think of a regular female name that started with the letter F, so she picked a different one. "Like Karen," she said.

Feather gave Megan a knowing look. "We both know that the name Karen comes with a lot of baggage because of all the internet memes. I imagine something like that would affect a person. It might affect a person a great deal." She shook her head. "What a terrible thing to do and to so many women. It's a popular name, or at least it was. People can be so cruel."

Megan ate one of the miniature cakes as well. It was too sweet. Megan wasn't like the self-proclaimed carboholics and chocoholics in the group. For her, there was such a thing as too much icing. Tea cakes were not just corner pieces, they were four corners' worth of icing.

Feather finished eating the cake then set out the sign-in book and fixed the chairs, adjusting each one with precision. It was such a Feather thing to do. Her chair circle was never lopsided. Her armpits were never dank. She was definitely the marrying type of girl, not just a for-now girl.

Feather said, "About your name… I think I might start calling you Megan instead of Meenie. Would you be comfortable with that?"

"Nah." Megan waved her hand. "It's too late. Everyone knows me as Meenie, and they might not know who you're talking to. Forget I brought it up. Never mind."

"For the record, I don't think you're mean," Feather said. She took a seat in her usual spot, with her back to the door, and crossed her legs. She quickly adjusted the loose-fitting sweater that fell down over the waist of her long skirt. It was a tiny gesture, but it gave away everything.

Megan gasped. "Holy smokes! You're pregnant, Feather! There's a bun in your oven! That's why you ate the cake before the meeting started. How far along are you?"

Feather glanced over her shoulder at the door to make sure they were alone. "Shh. It's not official. Please don't mention this because I'm not out of the woods yet. This one's going well so far, but… you know."

Megan patted her own stomach. "I don't know about babies, but I do own a baby maker, so I'm qualified to pretend I know. Don't worry, I won't tell the others."

Feather adjusted her sweater so her bump wasn't visible. "You're good at noticing things in other people. I hope you'll share something tonight about yourself, if you're ready."

"I could try, but you know I don't have major problems. I only come here for fun. I'm not a dumpster fire with a grease fire on top, like some of the others."

Feather gave Megan an amused smile. "Of course you're not a dumpster fire. I remember. You only came here that first night because you thought it was a weight loss group.”

“And I thought it must have been a good one, because there were so many skinny people in the group.”

Feather asked, “At what point did you realize it wasn’t a weight loss group?”

“Halfway through the meeting.”

Feather laughed. “But you kept coming.”

Megan shrugged. “I lost five pounds, so it worked. I used to stress-bake and eat everything myself, but then I started bringing the goodies here. When you find a system that works, you stick to it.”

“I’m glad you did. What did you think of the new guy last week? He signed in as Andrew, but he called himself Drew. I noticed you two had a little moment apart from the others.”

“He’s obviously a sex addict,” Megan said.

“Did he tell you that?”

“No. He lied and said he didn’t have any problems that he knew of.”

“This is a popular self-help group for people who claim to not have problems.”

Megan shrugged. “Folks keep coming back for the baking, I guess.”

The door creaked, and the rest of the members started filing in. People signed their names into Feather’s book so she could keep the billing straight. The therapist charged a small fee per drop-in, just to cover her time. The first few sessions were free. Compared to one-on-one therapy, it was a great deal. The only downside was sitting through other people wrestling with their problems and losing.

Megan kept an eye on the door, watching for Drew. He’d promised to come, so if he didn’t show up, that meant he was both a sex addict and a liar.

Abbie sat beside Megan. "That's certainly an interesting T-shirt. You've got a lot of guts, Meenie."

Megan looked down at her I Heart BJ shirt. "The initials stand for Beijing. The shirt says *I love Beijing*. It's not dirty unless it's being read by somebody with a dirty mind."

"Have you ever been to China?"

"No."

Abbie patted Megan's leg. "You don't have to lie to me, dear. I know what a B and J stand for." She pointed to her white hair. "There may be snow on the mountain, but there's fire below."

"You wild thing, Abbie."

"I wonder if that young man will come back tonight."

"Who?" Megan asked, playing dumb.

"Don't worry, dear. He's all yours. I won't fight you for him." Abbie pretended to claw the air between them.

"Oh, *that* guy," Megan said. "You can have him. He looks like the sensitive type. He probably cries at movies."

"There's nothing wrong with a man who's in touch with his emotions." Abbie waggled her white eyebrows. "If they're the *right* emotions."

Megan pretended to be horrified. "Abbie! Shame on you. The meeting for sex addicts is down the hall."

The door opened, and Drew came in, wearing an even nicer suit than the previous week.

"There he is," Abbie said. "Now there's a tall drink of water." She leaned in and whispered, "I wouldn't kick him out of bed for eating crackers."

"You bad girl," Megan said. "Full confession? I want to lick his entire face."

Abbie pulled away. "That's… interesting. Maybe keep that to yourself tonight."

"I'll try," Megan said.

She looked over at Drew.

He made eye contact, smiled, and settled back in his seat.

Chapter 7

Feather started the session and got right down to business. First up was Ryan.

Ryan said, "I went to the mall this weekend."

Feather asked, "How did that go?"

"I spent an hour going in circles because I couldn't get on the escalator. I did try. I got close a couple of times, but my heart started pounding, and I thought I was going to have a heart attack."

"That's what a panic attack feels like," Feather said. "Did you try the breathing techniques?"

"I got an ice cream," Ryan said. "And some caramel corn. And a burger."

Abbie said, "Oh, honey. It's not going to help your issues if you balloon up on all that junk food."

Feather said, "Sometimes a light snack can help us calm our system."

"I had more than a light snack," Ryan said. "On my fifth lap around the mall, I returned the jeans I had just bought. They were already snug when I tried them on, and I thought, oh what's the use? I'm hopeless."

"You're not hopeless," Feather said. "You have all of us, and we're hopeful for you."

"That's right," said Bald Guy Number Two.

Megan was only dimly aware of Ryan's story about the mall.

Normally, it would have been impossible for Megan to listen to Ryan's battle with the escalator without laughing. That night, it was a good thing—for Ryan and his phobias—that Megan was utterly consumed by staring at the new guy.

Drew certainly could wear a suit. It got even better when he casually untied the tie and took off his jacket, stripteasing for Megan without even knowing it. His easy, relaxed movements reminded Megan of a famous actor—someone like Dalton Deangelo—sitting down for an interview on a talk show.

Drew was out of place there. He was way too good-looking to be in group therapy, let alone with that group of misfits. Judging by the tailoring of the suit, he should have been paying for one-on-one.

In fact, in a way, it wasn't fair to the rest of the group that Drew was there, being so distracting. How were they supposed to focus on their problems when they were too busy mentally drooling over Drew's handsome, lickable face? Or finding themselves falling into those dazzling brown eyes?

Megan was feeling warm, even in just her light T-shirt. She kept getting warmer.

The hem of Drew's suit pants had ridden up enough to reveal his socks, and even his socks were appealing. They were argyle—those interlocking diamond shapes that had a suave, gentlemanly quality to them.

Megan tried to look at anything but Drew. It would be her turn to talk soon, and she didn't want to gibber like an idiot about Drew's socks. She looked at the floor. The floor was gray carpet tiles. Not appealing. Her eyes flicked back up to Drew. He was so much nicer to look at. Especially his socks and ankles. Were men's ankles sexy? They were when they were on Drew's body.

The group session kept going around until it reached Abbie, who was sitting next to Megan.

Abbie said, "I didn't see my sister in the last week, so I've got nothing to report." She turned to Megan. "Go ahead, dear."

Megan jerked up with surprise and said, "Oh, balls." All she could think about was Drew, his ankles, and his argyle socks. She covered her face with her hand and slumped down in her chair. "Somebody else go. I can't go. I, uh, don't have anything to say."

The retired librarian said, "That's a first."

Ryan said, "It's not that surprising. Meenie's only got something to say when it's someone else's turn."

Abbie put her arm around Megan's back. "I think she's just feeling a little shy because of the new person." She nodded at Drew.

There was a collective murmur in the group.

Out of the corner of her eye, Megan saw Drew pointing to his chest. "Me? I haven't done anything wrong, that I know of. But if you want me to leave, I'll leave."

Carla, who was in the group because she was grieving over her dog, said, "Young man, you shouldn't be bothering our Meenie."

Megan looked up in surprise. Carla didn't usually say much at all. She was worked up that night about something, and the culprit seemed to be the new guy.

Carla waved a crooked finger at Drew. "I saw you last week, Mr. Fancy Pants. I saw you putting your dirty moves on our Meenie last week. This isn't the group for sex addiction, you know."

Everyone looked to the group's leader.

Feather was holding her hand over her mouth. Her face was pale and waxy. It had to be the pregnancy, Megan thought. Morning sickness didn't just happen in the morning.

When Feather didn't speak up, the others began their usual chatter.

Abbie said, "I'd like to stop by the sex addict group sometime. Just to say hello."

"They're not as much fun as you'd think," Ryan said. "Trust me. I played tourist over there a couple times."

"Shame on you," said Bald Guy Number Two.

The retired librarian joined in, shaming Ryan for going to a group he wasn't part of.

"I could be addicted to sex," Ryan said. "There are worse things to be addicted to."

Carla said, "The new guy has been making sexy eyes at everyone. He should have to wear sunglasses."

The others fell into chaos, agreeing and disagreeing.

Drew made eye contact with Megan. "Don't come to my defense right away," he said sarcastically. "I enjoy having my reputation dragged through the mud."

Feather still wasn't saying anything, so Megan clapped her hands to get their attention.

"Guys, calm down," Megan said loudly. "Drew didn't do anything wrong last week." The group was quiet. "Drew *did* come over and talk to me last week, but he didn't put any dirty moves on me. I'm fine, honestly."

Drew raised his hand. "For the record, I'm not a sex addict," he said. "Not that there's anything wrong with that." He looked right at Ryan.

Ryan turned and looked behind himself.

One of the bald guys said to the woman next to him, "Methinks the gentleman doth protest too much."

One of the ladies murmured that she'd known a sex addict once, and he also wore a suit.

Megan made eye contact with Drew and mouthed the word *yikes.*

Drew leaned forward into the circle and said to Megan, though everyone else could also hear it, "You were here first. If my being here makes you unable to share, I can find another group. Just say the word, and I'll back off."

"You would?"

"Of course I would." He looked around at the others, meeting their eyes and charming them one by one with his undeniable charisma. "What does the group think? Should I leave?"

The others didn't answer and neither did Megan. There was a part of her that wanted to prove something by chasing him off. Doing so would prove that he wasn't worthy of staying. But there was another part of her that wanted him to stay. That part was her entire body.

One of the bald guys said, "I don't mind having a few more men around."

The other bald guy said, "It's good to get a male perspective on problems. No offense to the ladies."

"If Meenie's okay, I'm okay," Carla said. She narrowed her eyes at Drew. "But I will be keeping an eye on you, with your slick suits and your expensive haircut."

Drew said, "I want nothing more than what's best for the group." He shot a look across the circle at Megan. A look that said he *did* want more than what was best for the group.

Then he turned his handsome face toward Feather. "What next?"

Feather swallowed hard then fanned her face. She leaned forward in her seat. "Perhaps we should all take a short break."

There was a murmur of confusion. They never took a break in the middle of a session.

Abbie said, "There are tea cakes. Meenie must have brought them for us. They look delicious."

Carla said, "I suppose we could take a short break. Just this one time."

Feather held her fingers to her mouth, like she might throw up. She put her hand down slowly and rested it on her knee.

Drew said to Feather, concern in his voice, "I'll get you some water."

"No need," Feather said. "I'll go for a walk to the fountain in the hallway. All of you can take a break as well, or you can continue without me. It's your choice. Perhaps our newest member is ready to share something this week." She looked at Drew, then Megan, then got up and left the room, taking short, quick steps.

Ryan pointed to Feather's empty chair and said, "Command Central is open for a new Captain!"

Everyone laughed.

Abbie elbowed Megan then pushed her forward in her chair. "Meenie should take over," she said. "She likes being in control."

"I'll gladly take the wheel," Megan said. "But only if I get to crack open Drew's handsome skull and stir my wooden spoon around in his brain meat."

The others were supportive of the idea, if not of Megan's choice in wording.

Megan crossed the circle, took over Feather's chair, mimed writing on an imaginary notepad, and said, "Next, let's skip over a few people—don't worry, we'll come back to you guys—and let's hear what's going on with Drew."

Everyone turned to Drew expectantly.

"Well?" Megan prompted. "Why are you here? What's your damage, anyway?"

"You go first," he said. "What's your damage? Why are you here?"

"Easy one," Megan said. "I don't have any damage. I came here the first time because I thought it was a weight loss group, then I just stuck around."

Drew's dark, sexy eyes flitted down her face and over her body. "You don't need to lose weight. If anything, you could stand to put a little meat on those bones."

The group made an ooh sound, like the audience of a lively talk show.

Megan rolled her eyes and explained to the group, "Notice how he was giving me a negative comment paired with a compliment? Ladies, watch out for guys who do that." She pointed her thumb at Drew. "Classic player move. He must be a salesman. What do you think he sells? High-end luxury cars?"

"My guess is hot tubs," Carla said. "I knew a guy who looked like him, and he sold hot tubs."

Drew said to the group, "I'm not a salesman. Not that there's anything wrong with that." He said to Megan, "What do you do for a living, anyway?"

"Flowers," she said. "I'm a florist at Gardenia Flowers, over on Baker Street."

"So you're the salesperson," Drew said.

"The flowers sell themselves," Megan said. "We don't resort to your kind's style of smarmy high-pressure tactics."

"Are you accusing me of smarmy high-pressure tactics because last week I herded you like a sheep?"

"A little."

"That was an accident. I was hot and getting sweaty. When you had your back to me, I was trying to air out my armpits. When you turned around, I didn't want you to know what I was doing, so I pretended it was on purpose."

Across the circle, someone murmured, "That's a good share. Very honest."

Someone else asked, "How do you herd someone like sheep?"

Another person tried to explain what they'd seen Drew doing the previous week, and soon, everyone was talking at once. The meeting descended back into chaos.

Drew leaned forward to make eye contact with Megan and asked, "Is it usually like this?"

"It happens a lot," she said.

"Do people have… you know… emotional breakthroughs? Even with all of this going on?" He waved at the subgroup that was now practicing sheepherding on each other.

"I don't know about breakthroughs," Megan said. "I haven't had any, but I'm not here about any big problems."

"Of course not," Drew said. "You don't have any problems." He waved at her shirt. "You wear a provocative T-shirt like that because you're a completely well-adjusted person."

"A person who loves Beijing," she said.

"Have you been to China?"

"That's beside the point. Have you been sharing notes with Abbie?"

He held her gaze. "I want to know if you wore that shirt tonight on purpose to provoke me."

"You think I wore a provocative—*allegedly provocative*—shirt tonight for the sole purpose of provoking you? Why would I do that?"

"You tell me," he said.

"Not everything means something," Megan said. "I don't know why people always want a reason. If a plane crashes in the ocean, they want to know why. They need to find out which bolt was loose, because if there was no bolt loose, that means the universe is nothing but chaos. If there's no loose bolt and no terrorist plot, then nothing means anything. There's no story or narrative to bad things that happen, and then nothing makes sense, and most people can't handle that."

"Just because some things don't have answers, that doesn't mean we should give up," Drew said.

Now they were the only two seated in the circle. Everyone else was playing the sheepherding game or eating the miniature cakes.

"Is that what you're here for?" Megan sat back and crossed one leg loosely over the other. "Are you here for some sort of meaning? You know, there are plenty of churches in the area."

"First I'm a sex addict, and now I'm looking for a religion?"

"The two things aren't universally exclusive, from what I hear."

He looked over at the others. "Those cakes are disappearing fast."

"First you want to talk about my shirt, and now you want to talk about the cakes I made. You're obsessed with me. Admit it."

He gave her a half grin. "I wouldn't say I'm obsessed. Just curious."

"You should be curious about yourself and your own problems. That's what Feather always says. She says people who become curious about themselves make the most progress."

"And are you curious about yourself?"

"I already know who I am. What's there to be curious about?"

"So why'd you wear that T-shirt?"

"Why'd you wear that suit?"

"That's a good question. I could have gone home and changed before coming here, but I didn't. That might mean that, subconsciously, I always want to put my best foot forward."

"It's a nice suit, but I think a fun T-shirt with a logo or a slogan on it would tell people more about who you are." Megan pointed her finger at Drew. "*You* don't want people to know the real Drew. You'd rather hide behind your nice suit and your expensive haircut."

He looked down for a moment. "I do pay too much for my haircuts," he said.

"That was just a joke. I only said it because Carla brought it up. I like your hair."

"You like my hair?" He patted his head. "What else do you like about me?"

"Are you fishing for compliments? Don't you get enough at work, where everyone runs around trying to make you happy? You need to pay your staff more if you want them to really kiss your butt."

"I like *your* hair," he said. "And your eyes."

Megan narrowed her eyes at him. "Exactly how terrible at sex are you? I said I wasn't going home with you last week, but if you keep up the flattery, I might have to make an exception to my no-pretty-boys rule."

He looked away.

Feather, who'd returned unnoticed, placed a hand on Megan's shoulder. "Thanks for filling in for me," she said.

Megan waved at the others, who were paying no attention to their leader or substitute leader. "This group is uncontrollable. Look at them over there, mashing cake into their faces like lunatics. I don't know how you do this, week after week."

Feather said, "Drew, Megan, I've been standing here for a few minutes, observing you, and I need to talk to you both about something delicate."

Drew stared down at his hands, which he'd been doing since Megan had asked him how terrible he was in bed.

"Anyone can see that something is going on between you two," Feather said. "Both of you use humor to disarm people and deflect attention from yourselves. I think you two can help each other a lot, but… here's the delicate part. You can either date or be in the same group. Not both."

Megan's jaw dropped. "You're kicking us out of the group?"

Drew said nothing.

Feather said, "I've got to do something. The others might enjoy the show you put on, but that's all it will be. A show. For them. Not for yourselves."

"I'll go," Drew said. "It wasn't one of my best ideas to come here in the first place. It's only fair that I leave. Meenie was here first."

"Don't go," Megan said. "Drew, you can't go. You're the best part of this group."

"I am?"

Feather, who had one hand on Megan's shoulder, placed her other hand on Drew's shoulder. "I have an idea," she said. "You two can take a break from the larger group and try meeting regularly in a smaller group. A group that's just the two of you."

Megan asked, "What about the big group? Can we come back later, after things have fizzled out? Drew will need some help picking up the shattered pieces of his life."

Drew smirked. "Is that what you think will happen?"

"I take no prisoners," Megan said. "I offer no guarantee for safe passage aboard the S.S. Meenie."

"That's more than enough for now," Feather said. "Save it for your first miniature group session."

"You mean our first *date*," Megan said. "You want us to date, Feather. You're *ordering* us to date. Is that even something you're allowed to do? Don't you have a code of ethics about stuff like this?"

"Never mind my rules," Feather said. "Rules get bent sometimes. And I'm flexible. If you don't want to date, we could work something out where you alternate who comes to the group each week. So what's your decision? Dating or group?"

Megan looked into Drew's glinting brown eyes. "You go first," she said.

"Let's give our answers on the count of three," Drew said. "One. Two…"

Megan said, "Group."

Drew said, "Dating."

Megan shook her head. "I meant to say dating, same as you. Everyone's being so noisy over there, and they threw me off my game."

Drew said, "I was going to say group, but I didn't want to damage your fragile self-esteem."

"Then I'm changing my answer back," Megan said. "We'll do shared custody of the group. Unless…"

Drew leaned forward in his chair, his expression hopeful and a bit smug.

"Unless you think we should go on one or two dates," Megan said. "Just to make Feather happy. Feather does so much for the group. You'd know that if you were a regular and not a sightseer."

"I'd go on a few dates with you," he said. "To make Feather happy."

Feather shook her head. "You two have so much work to do."

Megan threw her hands up. "Not me! My work is done. I already lost my five pounds. I don't have any real problems. I know who I am, and I'm perfectly happy."

"Me too," Drew said. "Who wouldn't want to be me? I love being me. I'm the best."

Megan pointed her finger at Drew. "Narcissist!"

Drew frowned. "I do know what that is, and I'm not a narcissist. Maybe you are."

"Easy with the labels," Feather said. "People aren't labels." She dropped her hands from their shoulders and took a step back. "I think that's enough for tonight. Now, if you don't mind, I'm going to round everyone up to resume the session. Let's see if we can't help the people who aren't already perfect, like you two."

Drew asked, "Should we leave now?"

Feather said, "You can stay until the end of the session. It would be more disturbing to the group if you left halfway. While you're here, try to… I mean, try *not* to… oh never mind."

Chapter 8

It was late when Megan got home from the meeting. She'd stayed behind to flirt with Drew and exchange numbers but nothing more. Feather had stood there through all of it, like a chaperone.

The lights were still on at Tina's cottage in the backyard. Megan parked her mother's Cadillac behind Tina's car in the alley.

The alley was lined with cars because many of the homeowners in the neighborhood had rented out their basements or converted their garages into rentals. When Megan had been a little kid, riding her bike up and down the alley, there weren't any cars parked back there. Things changed, whether you wanted them to or not.

Megan knocked on her sister's door, which felt unnecessary and wrong. Megan was used to walking right in or using the spare key if the door was locked, but two weeks ago, she'd gotten an eyeful by accident. Tina and Luca had been playing more than Scrabble. The passage of two weeks' time hadn't erased the visual from Megan's brain.

Luca had broken his foot at the Baker Street Block Party, and now it was in a cast. He'd been around Tina's cottage a lot. The man kept motorcycles parked on the main floor of his house while the living quarters were upstairs. He could have hobbled up his own stairs if he wanted to, but he preferred staying with Tina. He probably didn't want her to get away from him again.

Megan banged on the door again, right as it opened.

Tina's cheeks were flushed, but she was wearing clothes. Megan peered around her sister. Luca Lowell was there, sitting on the L-shaped couch.

Lucas and his large, roast-beef-devouring body made the enormous sofa look relatively small.

The sisters exchanged playful pleasantries. Tina wasn't terribly welcoming.

"Come in," Luca said, playing the good cop to Tina's bad cop. "We're just playing Scrabble."

Megan joined them in the living room, which was also the entire room. The couch they were sitting on folded out into a bed, and the only other room was the bathroom.

Megan glanced around, tallying up the extra clutter that belonged to Luca: laptop, manly jeans, manly boots, and manly sweaters with chunky buttons. There was a lot of manly stuff inside the tiny cottage.

"You guys could take over the big house if you want," Megan told them, generously offering a swap for the second or third time that month. "It's just me and Muffins over there, and we can totally trade while you're in that cast."

Tina slipped another pillow under Luca's white cast then tickled his exposed toes affectionately. "We're cozy," she said.

"Couldn't be cozier," Luca said.

"I see you have wine," Megan said.

Tina jumped up, grabbed a wine glass from the kitchen, and filled it for Megan.

"You're a good sister," Megan said before taking a long sip. "Ooh, this is my favorite kind," she said of the wine.

"You like pinot grigio?" Luca asked while clearing the Scrabble board to start over with three players.

Megan grinned at the guy she assumed would be her future brother-in-law. "My favorite kind of wine is *free* wine."

Luca laughed at the joke.

Tina groaned. "Luca, everyone in our family says that, at every single Thanksgiving or Christmas dinner. It's so corny."

Luca gave Tina a sappy look, as if to say he couldn't wait to spend every family dinner with Tina and her family, even Meenie, who really wasn't as bad as everyone said she was.

Tina gave Luca a sappy look back. Megan got the distinct impression she'd interrupted some important business, and it hadn't been Scrabble.

A more conscientious person might have left the couple to their privacy but not Megan. She pawed through her Scrabble tiles, gulped the rest of the wine, and waved for a refill, which Tina ignored.

"The service here is lacking," Megan said as she refilled the glass herself. "No tip."

Tina swatted her on the arm.

The three chatted about the wine for a bit. Luca had a wine cellar, which was a fact he liked to drop into conversations as much as possible.

Megan kept looking at Tina and Luca, observing the energy between them. She was struggling to find her equilibrium in this new arrangement of two against one. How was this going to work? Now that Luca and Tina were together, had Megan gained a friend in Luca or lost her best friend to a man?

She desperately wanted to talk to Tina about all the new feelings she was having but not necessarily in front of Luca. Megan wished Luca didn't have to be there all the time. Megan was happy for her sister, but the guy *did* have a big house across town. He needed to clear out all the motorbikes or get an elevator or something.

During the chat, Luca said to Megan, "Your self-help group sounds interesting. Tina told me about it. I hope you don't mind."

"It's not a secret, you big dummy," Megan said.

Tina kicked Megan in the shin. "Behave yourself."

"I'm sorry," Megan said to Luca. *Sorry you're dumb*, she finished in her head.

Tina asked, "What's gotten into you tonight?"

"There's a new guy in the group," Megan told them and gave a brief rundown about Drew and the situation.

Tina gave her sister a skeptical look.

Megan carried on anyway. "Can you believe it? I may have finally found someone who's got enough man parts to take a few jokes," she said. "And he's not bad on the eyeballs. Whenever I look at him, he really fires up my engines, on all the cylinders." She gave Luca a meaningful look. "Dude, you know what I'm talking about. Vroom vroom."

She went on about how good-looking Drew was and how he compared to Luca.

Luca kept looking away out of embarrassment. He might have run away, if he didn't have a cast on his foot, and if there was anywhere else to go in the tiny house.

Megan took another big glug of the wine. "This is pretty good for free wine."

"Because it wasn't free, and it didn't come out of a box like Aunt Jane's wine," Tina said. "Are we going to meet this guy? Maybe we should go on a double date. Luca and I can chaperone."

Luca made a strangled sound.

Tina shot him a look.

Luca gulped and said, "Sure. Double date. We can chaperone. That sounds like a great idea." His tone said otherwise.

Tina asked, "What's his last name? What does he do for a living? How old is he?"

"I don't know any of those things, but I'm going to find out," Megan said. "Feather ordered us to date each other. She basically deputized me to be his new personal therapist."

Tina's jaw dropped. "What?"

Megan explained to Luca, "Feather is our group's leader. She's got a license to stir around people's brains. She said that Drew and I had an electric sexual tension that was going to make the group explode into a kinky sex cult situation if we didn't do something to pop the tension."

Tina said, "I'm sure she didn't say that."

"It's basically what she meant, though," Megan insisted.

Luca wisely kept his mouth shut.

Tina asked, "What did she *really* say? There's no way she told two people at her group they had to quit the group to date each other. That wouldn't be ethical."

"Oh, but she did. I guess it was technically more of a prescription than an order. Is that the right word? Prescription?" She looked over at Luca. She was having trouble with the pronunciation of the word *prescription* and wasn't even sure it was a word. It had been hours since she'd eaten, and the wine was hitting her like bathtub moonshine at a prom.

Luca raised his eyebrows. "Sounds like you've had quite the day," he said. "Things might seem different tomorrow morning, when you sober up."

"I'm not drunk," Megan said. "If you think this is me drunk, you ain't seen nothin' yet."

"You should probably take your therapist's advice," Tina said. "By which I mean the *actual* advice she gave you, not this crazy idea you got in your head that she ordered you two to date each other."

"I was there, Teenie," Megan said. "I heard what she said, with my own ears, and so did Drew. We *have to* date each other. It's the only way. The only option." She left out the offer Feather made that they share custody of the group instead.

Tina shook her head. "This guy sounds like trouble."

"I disagree," Luca said. "Fate put this guy in your path for a reason," he said to Megan, his expression earnest. "Fate can lead you to the trough, like a horse, but it can't make you drink. I know I'm mixing metaphors here, but meeting him by fate won't mean anything if you don't take a chance. A person has to take chances, or they never get anything."

Megan waved her drink at Luca's face. "You're one of those barstool philosopher guys, aren't you? You're like a therapist who's a slot machine, except you take wine instead of quarters."

Luca's bright-blue eyes were lively. "Maybe it's the wine, but I kind of get what you're saying," he said.

"Dude, you're an old soul with the right sort of face," Megan said. "I like how your face looks when I'm talking, Luca. I especially like that your mouth stays shut. That's a good quality in a person."

"I've been told I'm a good listener," he said. "Why don't you start over at the beginning and tell us everything that happened at your group?" He hobbled over to the tiny kitchen and produced another bottle of wine as if by magic.

Tina sighed.

Megan glared at her sister. "Luca's being a better big sister than you are right now." She yelled at Luca, even though he was only five feet away, "Did you hear that? I said you're a great big sister!"

Luca said, "I'll take that as a compliment." He grinned. "Little sister."

Tina rolled her eyes and started organizing her Scrabble tiles for what would be a long night of arguing over words, scoring, and how big a disaster dating Drew was going to be.

Chapter 9

Wednesday

Muffins stomped across the bed, his white socks hammering the duvet like elephant feet. He lowered his whiskered chin to Megan's and then battered her like a rutting mountain goat until she finally got up to feed him.

Megan was brewing tea when Luca stopped by, without Tina. The older Gardenia sister had gone to open the flower shop, and Luca had the morning free.

"You're quiet this morning," Luca said.

"Someone got me drunk last night so they could cheat at Scrabble."

"Is that what happened?" He elbowed her out of the way and started brewing a pot of his favorite coffee. Tina's tiny cottage didn't have a decent coffee maker, so Luca had been coming around the main house for his fix lately.

Megan asked, "When does the cast come off? I bet the inside of it smells *so* bad."

"If they let me keep the cast, I'll bring it over here so you can smell it."

"They'd *better* let you keep it. That cast is a work of art." Megan had been drawing crude cartoons all over the cast. Some of the guys who worked at Luca's garage had tried to one-up her with their own artwork. Luca needed to cover it with a sock when he went out in public.

"We'll see," he said. "Do you happen to know Tina's ring size?"

Megan nearly dropped her mug of tea. "Shut up! No you aren't!"

He gave her a bashful look. "You're not going to ruin the surprise, are you?"

"Of course not, you big dummy. I didn't tell her I went with you to pick out those charms for her bracelet, did I?"

"You're a woman of your word," he said. "Thanks again."

"I won't tell her, but only as long as you bring me with you to shop for engagement rings. It might be the only time in my life I get to try on a diamond."

"Don't say that," he said. "You're young. What are you, twenty-five?" He scratched his stubbly chin. "I should know how old you are. My brain's running a bit slow from last night."

"I'm twenty-eight," she said.

"Still young," he said.

"I'm practically an old maid. I already have one cat. I just need a dozen more, and I'll be set up as a crazy cat lady."

Muffins, who had spectacular timing, meowed just then.

Megan bent down and patted the cat. "Don't worry, Muffmeister. You'll always be my number one man."

Luca asked, "When are you having your first date with the guy? Derek?"

"You mean Drew," she said. "Friday. We're meeting at O'Flannigan's."

"Don't you mean O'Hannigan's?"

"Ah, classic mistake. The letter F and the letter L were put too close together on the sign, so people think it's an H, but it's not."

"The place isn't called O'Hannigan's?"

"Have a closer look the next time you go in. Gary Jackson is always spouting off about people getting the name wrong, but he's too cheap to get the sign fixed."

"The man is cheap," Luca said.

"And he bans people from the pub for no good reason," Megan said. "For months at a time." She waved her hand and repeated, "For no good reason!"

"That's not what I heard," Luca said calmly.

"You're new. You'll figure things out eventually."

Luca poured cream into his coffee and stirred it up. "I'm busy Friday night, so I'm afraid I can't chaperone you two."

"We don't need a chaperone," Megan said. "Did Tina say we did? I'll kill her."

"It's not the worst idea," he said. "Do you have another friend or two you can invite along with you? Dates don't always have to be limited to just two people. Sometimes it's easier to relax with other people are around. It takes off the pressure."

"What if I like pressure?"

Luca snorted. "I know *you* like pressure, but what if it's too much for this Drew guy? You want to get through a reasonable number of dates before you make any serious decisions. Maybe four or five dates. You can start off with something casual."

"Dude, there was *nothing* casual about you selling off all our flowers so my sister had to go for breakfast with you. It was practically an ambush situation."

"Okay. Don't take my dating advice."

"No. Maybe you have a point," she said, hopping up on the counter to steer clear of Luca's foot cast and his clumsy one-legged hopping. "I should bring a friend so they can back me up, then it will be two against one. Drew won't know what hit him."

"That's not quite what I meant."

"I'll bring Tina."

"She's busy Friday night. We have plans for the weekend."

"Then I'll have to bring one of my other friends."

"Like who? Come to think of it, I don't know your friends, except for the ones who are also friends with Tina."

Megan looked down and flicked some crumbs off the counter. She didn't want to admit that Tina was her best friend and practically the only one. Most of the other girls Megan used to hang out with had moved on with their lives and weren't interested in hanging out with Megan. And the guys she was friends with, well, most of them had a history with her that would have made bringing them along to a date beyond awkward.

When Megan didn't answer right away, Luca said, "I could change around our weekend plans. We could leave Saturday morning so we're still here Friday night. We'll go to O'Hannigan's or O'Flannigan's with you, kiddo." He reached up his big hand and patted Megan's head.

She pulled away, pretending she didn't like it. "Don't be a big dummy," she said. "I can go on a date by myself."

"But wouldn't you feel more relaxed if you had someone else there?"

"Like a therapy cat?" Megan stared at him. "Feather did mention that some people benefit from therapeutic animals. I could bring Muffins."

"I'm not sure that's a good idea."

"Don't get your panties in a bunch," Megan said. "That was just a joke. I'll bring Rory."

"Rory Taylor?"

"That's the one. She's friends with me too. She's not just Teenie's friend."

"You must be kidding. Rory can barely be around me, and I'm under strict orders not to kiss, touch, or even look fondly at Tina when we're hanging out with her."

"It must be hard for you to keep your hands to yourself."

"It is, but Rory's Tina's best friend. I respect her boundaries."

"Exactly," Megan said. "Rory's the perfect person to bring on a date because of the boundaries."

"Hmm." Luca leaned back against the counter and crossed one arm over his muscular stomach as he lifted his coffee to his lips. "There's no way Rory Taylor will go on a date with you and Drew."

Megan knew the sound of a gauntlet being thrown. She lifted her chin defiantly. "Challenge accepted."

Chapter 10

Friday

Megan Gardenia scanned the murky darkness of the pub known to most as O'Flannigan's but known to some people as O'Hannigan's.

She spotted the first party to arrive for the Friday-night date. Rory Taylor. There would be three of them in total. Rory liked to get to places early so she could choose the optimal seat.

Rory sat at a raised table in the corner, her back to the wall for safety. Her eyes were fixed on the flickering votive candle before her. She wore her dark curly hair loose around her shoulders. Rory had beautiful curls with a natural streak of white. She was always threatening to shave her head because she went nuts over the idea of getting a hair in her food. When she was feeling good enough to wear her hair down, it meant she was feeling relaxed, which made Megan feel relaxed.

Megan trotted over to the table and loudly exclaimed, "You must be my date! Wow! You look just like your photo!"

Rory's eye twitched. "Are you going to behave, or are you in one of your weird moods?"

"Does it matter? I'm paying for your dinner, so suck it up."

As Luca had predicted, Rory had not been eager to accompany Megan on her date with Drew. However, Megan was not one to back down from a challenge. It turned out Rory only required a small amount of arm-twisting and guilt-tripping to agree. When Megan rubbed her victory into Luca's face at a future time, she would leave out the part where she got down on her knees and begged.

Megan picked up the menu that was already on the table and checked the specials insert. "How was your day? You had that snooty auction job, right? Where the rich ladies bid on paintings they don't like, for charity? They buy some abstract thing that doesn't match the sofa, and they act like they're personally curing the world's hunger crisis, right?"

Rory's face lit up. "They loved the tea cakes. We got booked for three more jobs, right on the spot. I'm going to be really busy for a while." Rory loved being busy with work.

Drew wasn't there yet, so the girls ordered a first round of drinks. Rory wasn't sure she wanted anything, so Megan took charge and ordered a bottle of pinot grigio, largely because she loved saying pinot grigio, the new term she'd learned from Luca, the bike mechanic who owned a wine cellar.

Megan looked over the food menu, planning ahead. "Rory, they have your favorite."

"Nachos?"

"No." Megan leaned in. "Linguini."

Rory squirmed. She couldn't say the word linguini because it sounded dirty to her. If she ordered it that night, she would be pointing to the menu and calling them "those noodles." That was Rory Taylor. She couldn't say it, but she would eat it.

"Linguiiiiiini," Megan said, savoring the word. "I do love a good linguini. Don't you?"

"I don't know why I let you talk me into coming here," Rory said.

"Because I begged you on my knees," Megan said. "Plus you owe me."

"I don't owe you," Rory said. "I made a promise, which is different."

Rory *didn't* owe Megan anything, but Rory had bailed on the self-help group after just one visit.

Megan had been upset about it, claiming that the group's feelings were hurt by the rejection. Rory had promised to try something else in the future when Megan suggested it, and Megan cashed in that promise for tonight's date.

A tall, refined man with dark hair approached the table. He wore a business casual ensemble that wasn't a suit but was still three levels dressier than what any of the other men in O'Flannigan's/O'Hannigan's were wearing.

"Drew!" Megan exclaimed, jumping up. "I didn't recognize you with clothes on!"

Drew looked from Megan to Rory then back again. "You must be Tina," he said, offering Rory his hand.

"I'm actually the undocumented third sister," she said. "Not Tina."

"You're the what?"

Rory stood enough to reach across the table and shake his hand. "I'm a friend of the family. My name's Rory. Like Cory but with an R."

"Did you say you were the undocumented third sister?"

"It's just a joke," Rory said. "Lois Gardenia didn't actually adopt me."

"That's funny," Drew said. "In our family, we have something similar with Candy."

Both Rory and Megan gave Drew a blank look. They both thought he'd meant candy with a lowercase C, not Candy as in a person's name. Who was named Candy? Besides strippers.

Drew pulled out a chair and sat across from Rory, next to Megan.

"Is this a double date?" Drew asked. "Are we expecting one more, or is this it?"

Megan said, "This is it. Rory is our chaperone."

Drew raised his eyebrows. "Did Feather set this up?"

"This wasn't Feather's doing," Megan said. "Don't blame me. It was all my sister's boyfriend's idea. He said we should bring someone else along to help deflect some of the insane sexual tension that's always brewing between us."

In the corner, Rory made a strangled sound. She kicked Megan under the table.

Drew grinned. "Is that what this feeling is?"

"I have that effect on men," Megan said.

There was another kick from Rory.

Drew explained to Rory, "When Meenie said she didn't recognize me with my clothes on, it's because she's only seen me in a suit."

Rory, her gaze fixed on the votive candle, said, "I know. I heard all about it. Trust me."

Megan leaned over and whispered in Drew's ear, "My friend is very shy, so do me a solid and dial your sex magic down about three notches, will ya?"

He whispered back, "Did I do something wrong?"

"Not yet, but she's really squeamish."

"How squeamish?"

"Ask her if the linguini is any good, and you'll see."

Drew pulled away and pointed a finger at Megan. "Gotcha," he said. "It's all clear as mud. In my line of work, we pay a lot of attention to body language."

"What's mine saying?"

"I'm not sure. You're not that easy to read."

The waitress arrived with the wine. She'd brought an extra glass for Drew, who said he was happy to share the bottle.

Some big, beefy guys filed by the table on their way to the pool and darts area. They stopped to say hello to Drew. A guy with red hair kept looking at Megan and slapping Drew on the back.

After the guys left, Megan said, "I thought you told me you'd never been to this pub before."

Drew said, "I haven't. I know some of those guys from my old rugby days." He rubbed his shoulder. "Those were some crazy times."

"Rugby," Megan said. "That's a lot of body contact, huh? A lot of athletic dudes, slamming into each other over and over. Sounds like my kind of thing."

Rory kicked at Megan under the table, but she'd already moved her shins away.

Drew asked, "Are either of you rugby fans?"

"I'm more of a wrestling fan," Megan said.

Drew turned to Rory. "What about you?"

"I don't play sports," she said. "But I do watch. Did Meenie tell you she was on the wrestling team in high school?"

"She did not," he said to Rory. "I like having a chaperone," he said to Megan. "I've gotten more background information on you in five minutes than I did at two group sessions."

"You should have asked questions instead of herding me into a corner and groping me with your eyes."

"I tried," he said. "So, wrestling? Why am I not surprised?"

Over in the corner, Rory snorted. For all the fuss she'd made, she was enjoying the entertainment.

Drew said, "This is interesting. Tell me something. Did you trash-talk the other guys before and after you pinned them down?"

"I only wrestled girls."

Rory, who must have been feeling bolder after a few laughs and sips of wine, said, "That's not entirely true. She wrestled a few guys. She held them down until they cried."

"Some of my finest moments," Megan said, lifting her chin.

"I should warn you about something," Drew said. "I don't scare easily, and I do lift weights."

Megan reached over and squeezed his biceps. They were bigger than she'd expected. He'd been hiding them under loose-fitting shirts and suit jackets.

"Not bad," she said. "But strength isn't everything." She pulled her hand away. "Now stop being so flirty. You're going to make poor Rory's head pop off."

"I'm fine, you guys," Rory said. "But I've got to be up early, so I think I'll call it a night." She stood and reached for her coat.

"No dinner?" Megan asked. "No buttery pasta noodles?" Megan was proud of herself that she'd restrained herself from saying *linguini*. She really was on her best behavior tonight. Having a chaperone was working.

"You two have a nice first date," Rory said. "Drew, it was really good to meet you. If you ever need a caterer, call my company." She handed him a card.

"I might do that," he said. "My brother takes after my mom, and he's always throwing the most lavish dinner parties. Does your company do ice sculptures?"

"We have some contacts that do," Rory said. "Do you like swans?"

"Who doesn't?" Drew put the card into his wallet. "Thanks for coming along tonight. I enjoyed meeting you, Rory. I hope I'll see you again sometime."

Rory looked at Megan as she said, "I hope so too."

They said goodbye, and then Rory left.

Drew turned his head and watched as Rory walked away.

Megan grabbed his chin and tilted his face back toward hers. "If you look at Rory's butt one more time, I will take you down."

Their chaperone had been gone for all of five seconds, and already things had taken a turn.

Drew shook his chin away from Megan's grasp. "What? I wasn't—"

"Dude, if you look at another girl's butt when we're on a date together, you'll be eating peanut shells off the pub's carpet. And there's something else you should know. They haven't served peanuts here in five years. That's how far into the floor I'll shove your face."

He blinked. "I've never wanted to kiss a woman as badly as I do now."

Megan was speechless. This was not the reaction she normally got from guys, let alone the ones who looked like Drew.

Finally, she found her faculties and said, "Well? What are you waiting for? An engraved invitation?"

He slowly moved his chair so he was close enough to reach, then he touched his fingers to her cheek and kissed her. Tenderly.

Drew and Megan's chaperone hadn't even reached the door to exit the pub, and already, Drew and Megan were kissing.

Chapter 11

O'Flannigan's pub disappeared, like someone put the whole world on mute.

Drew's lips were just as kissable as they looked. His kisses could probably stop wars and lead humanity into a new golden age of enlightenment.

Megan might have melted into him or at least kept kissing him until she got kicked out of O'Flannigan's—again—but she managed to keep some non-reptilian part of her brain alert thanks to one key thought: *pepperoni*.

While Megan and Drew kissed, Megan repeated the word *pepperoni* in her brain, over and over. When the word alone wasn't enough, she tried to imagine that, under his nice business casual shirt, Drew didn't have regular male nipples but giant slices of pepperoni where they should have been. It was distracting and nonsexual enough that she was able to pull away and stop kissing his kissable lips.

"Pepperoni," she said out loud.

He gave her a stunned look. "You make a strong, albeit abbreviated, point," he said. "We should probably order some food. This wine is going to our heads."

She reached for the glass of ice water with lemon that the waitress had brought with the wine.

"Use this to cool yourself down." She dropped a chunk of ice onto Drew's lap.

He flicked the ice away and gave her a dirty look.

She did it again.

"Cut it out," he said, sounding annoyed.

"I didn't do it," she said. "Not on purpose. My hand does weird stuff sometimes, on its own. I think my hand might have Tourette's."

"That's not a thing."

"How do you know? Are you a doctor?"

"Yes. As a matter of fact, I am a doctor."

"Shut up. You are not."

"I have a certificate."

"Where?"

"At my dental practice."

"You're a dentist?" She dropped another chunk of ice on his lap. "A dentist isn't a real doctor."

"But I am a doctor. I'm Dr. Morgan."

She shook her head. "No way. That can't be your last name. If I married you, I'd be Megan 'Meenie' Morgan."

He gave her a funny look. "Tonight is certainly a fascinating journey into how your brain works."

"I don't believe you're a doctor or a dentist. I want to see certification."

"I've got some documents at my place. Do you want to go there with me?"

"To your place? For one night of mediocre sex? No thank you."

He smiled, which was not the reaction she expected. "Who said it'll be mediocre? I'm a bit rusty. It's been two full years, but I'm sure it's like riding a horse."

"You mean *bicycle*. It's like riding a bicycle."

"Bicycle. Horse. What's the difference?"

"Why haven't you been on a bicycle in two years?"

"Long story," he said. "Bad breakup." He frowned. "I guess that wasn't such a long story after all."

"Is that why you came to the group? Because you wanted to get over a bad breakup?"

"That wasn't why I went to the group. I just sort of wandered in by accident."

"But you stayed."

He shrugged. "My life wasn't going that well, so I figured I had nothing to lose. Group therapy seems pointless, but I figured things couldn't get any worse."

His words sunk in gradually, and a darkness rose within Megan. Her mouth, which had been sweet from the wine and kissing, turned sour.

Slowly, she said, "Let me get this straight, Dr. Drew Morgan. You want to take me back to your place on the pretense of showing me your doctor certificate because you've got nothing to lose?"

"I'm not trying to take you anywhere," he said.

"But you're hanging out with me because your life can't get any worse?" Her voice was cold, like a parking meter in the dead of winter.

He didn't pick up on the chill.

He did not pick up on it *at all*.

Rather than salvage the date with something sensible, he said, "And also because you're beautiful, Meenie." If only he hadn't used the word *and*. If only he'd said no to what she'd said and clarified, but he hadn't. He'd said that his life was bad, things couldn't get much worse, *and* she was beautiful.

Megan replied tersely, "You're only saying that because I'm a girl."

"I'm saying it because you are beautiful. And I think maybe you're my type."

She narrowed her eyes and crossed her arms. "You mean *easy*?"

"Complicated." He looked around at the pub, which was filling up with the Friday-night crowd. "Let's get out of here, Complicated Girl. It's noisy. I can't hear you that well. We can go dancing or get coffee or find a bowling alley. Let's get out of here and do something. Just the two of us. No chaperone."

She kept her arms crossed, her defenses up. "Let me get this straight, Dr. Drew Morgan. You went through a bad breakup two years ago, and you haven't slept with anyone since then?"

"Basically."

"And you think you're going to break your dry spell thanks to me?"

"Why not? We're both consenting adults. We even have our therapist's blessing."

She picked up her glass of ice water and threw it in his face.

"Ow!" He shook his head.

"Don't be a baby. I didn't hurt you."

"You got me in the eye with the lemon wedge!"

"You're lucky we're in public," she said. "If we weren't in the middle of a respectable establishment, I'd stick that lemon wedge somewhere a lot more intimate."

Any outsiders, such as the people sitting a few tables away, could see that things were not going well on the date.

Dr. Drew Morgan, however, was not at his most perceptive.

He'd gotten used to attributing Megan's brash talk to teasing. He assumed she was only joking about stuffing the lemon wedge somewhere. A person could hardly blame Drew for the mistake. Things had turned on the couple rather rapidly.

Drew squinted at Megan in what he thought was a playful manner. "I'd like to see you try," he said of the lemon wedge.

She threw a beer coaster at him, then she stormed out. She didn't need to grab her purse or go back to it, because Megan Gardenia kept her wallet in her back pocket, like a sensible human.

He yelled after her, "Meenie! What did I do?"

Megan didn't hear or see what happened next.

An older man with no hair came over to Drew and put his hand on Drew's shoulder. It was Jim, from the self-help group at the community center. He was the man Megan referred to as Bald Guy Number Two.

Jim said, "I don't know what you did, young man, but bless your heart for trying with that girl."

"You saw that?"

"I saw everything," Jim said. "I'm afraid that one's a lost cause."

"You're from the group at the community center," Drew said, finally placing the man's familiar face.

"I'm Jim." They shook hands.

Drew said, "You can join me if you'd like. I think the other chairs are still dry."

Jim sat down and handed Drew a cloth handkerchief from his pocket. "It's clean," he said. "I keep two of them on me at all times."

"That's very thoughtful and hygienic," Drew said. He wiped the water off his face. One eye was still watering from the lemon wedge.

Jim said, "Now, I know we're not supposed to talk about the group outside of the group, and I know we're not supposed to give up on people, but I don't think that girl is going to come around. Not until her next lifetime."

"You'd probably know better than I do, being part of that group."

"Cheer up," Jim said. "There are plenty of fish in the sea."

Drew didn't cheer up. The sea was large, and he'd been on it for two years with nothing to show for his time. He liked Megan.

Jim said, "Do you like fishing, Drew?"

Chapter 12

Saturday

Megan Gardenia was feeling blue when she opened Gardenia Flowers on Saturday morning. The bluest blue. She had the blues, and like a certain blues song—or maybe several of them—said, those blues were cutting to the bone.

She put an all-blues playlist on the shop's stereo then stepped inside the walk-in flower cooler to chill her thoughts. It was always easier to think under the hum of the condenser, in the cool air that kept the flowers in near-stasis. Whenever she was standing inside the cooler, she liked to imagine she was on a spaceship, inside a stasis pod, heading somewhere better.

The previous night's debacle with Drew kept playing on repeat in her head.

Despite what she'd said, she really *had* wanted to go home with him. She would have looked at his dentist certification, then they would have had some of that mediocre sex he was offering. It would have been bad but better than the zero sex she'd been getting.

What she did do, after she left the O'Flannigan's, was stop by the grocery store. She bought half a roasted chicken and three kinds of chips, plus dip. Megan's sister, Tina, had a sweet tooth and went on candy binges when she needed a mood boost. Megan hit the savory aisle.

When Megan got home, she sat on the floor in the kitchen and shared the chicken with Muffins. She'd gotten the plain kind, with no garlic seasoning, on account of him.

Then she hit rock bottom. For Megan, rock bottom was sobbing and blubbering to Muffins about him being "the only man who loves me, and that's just because I have free-range chicken." Then she used his soft orange fur to soak up her tears.

Now she was standing inside a walk-in flower cooler, wishing it were a spaceship stasis pod. She pressed her face against the interior glass in an attempt to press down the puffy bags under her eyes.

She could tell by the reaction of the customers walking into the flower shop that this was not what they were expecting, much less what they wanted.

With a heavy heart, Megan stepped out of the cooler and tried to be professional. She had to help an excited bride-to-be pick out wedding flowers.

Megan felt she did a decent job with the woman, considering Megan would never—cue the cat-fur-soaking sobs—know the joy of being a beautiful bride herself.

She got through the day with no meltdowns and was feeling better by closing time. She'd had to work the full shift so Tina could do romantic stuff all weekend with Luca. They'd gone to a fancy spa a few hours away to get a couples' massage from someone named Big Danny the Manny. It sounded suspicious as heck to Megan, but she figured that whomever those two paid to rub their backs was their business.

Tina phoned in from the spa at closing time to make sure Megan had everything under control.

"What would you do if I didn't have everything under control?" Megan asked. "You're not even in town."

"I'd figure out something," came the reassuring voice on the phone. "I'm your big sister, Meenie. It's my job to look out for you, especially while Mom's out of the country."

"In that case, I'd like a raise in my allowance."

"You don't get an allowance."

"Then I want a raise in my wages. I've got big purple bags under my eyes. I need to buy some face masks. I hear you can get some that are made out of snails."

"Megan," Tina said, using her serious tone and Megan's real name. "Rory told me you dragged her along with you to meet this Drew guy last night at O'Flannigan's."

"What did Rory tell you?"

"Just that he seemed nice. I think she liked him. Not for herself but for you. How did it go after she left?"

"About average."

Tina sighed into the phone line. "I'm sorry to hear that."

"We were alone about thirty seconds, and he started being very rude."

"I'm sorry to hear that." She didn't ask for details.

Megan knew what was going on. Tina thought she knew what had happened. Tina thought Megan had ruined the date, not Drew.

"Is that all you have to say?" Megan heard the agitation in her voice as her anger rose. "You're giving up on me and Drew after one bad date? If you and Luca had given up after one fight, where would you be now? You wouldn't be making googly eyes at each other while you get a couples' massage from Big Danny the Manny."

A moment passed, then Tina said, "If you want to go on a second date with Drew, go for it. Be my guest. I'm not stopping you."

Megan let her anger go with a defeated sigh. "He probably won't see me again," she admitted. "Not after I threw a drink in his face."

"You threw a drink in his face," Tina repeated. She didn't sound surprised, and she still didn't ask for details. "Hang in there," she said. "There's someone for everyone."

"That's what pretty people say to ugly people."

"What are you talking about? We're sisters, and we're practically identical. How can you say I'm pretty and you're ugly?"

"My nose is crooked, and one of my eyes is higher than the other."

"Meenie, love always makes us feel vulnerable and not good enough. I thought Luca was way out of my league. I still do. But he wants to be with me, so who knows? Maybe guys aren't half as critical as we think they are."

"But what do they want from us? Besides sex."

"Most of them want someone to be vulnerable with. There's a lot of pressure on guys to be tough and rugged, and they all give each other a hard time. Take Luca, for example. He was raised by his father, with no women around for most of his life. All those nice things that we girls do for each other we take for granted. Guys aren't like that, but they crave it."

"They do?"

"I bought Luca some big wool socks so he could wear one over his cast and keep his toes warm now that it's getting chilly. Then I helped him pull the sock on. When I looked up at his face, he looked like he was going to cry or propose to me or both." She chuckled softly. "He's a big sweetie."

Megan said, "I could buy someone a pair of warm woolly socks."

"Would Drew like a pair of warm woolly socks?"

Megan snorted. She'd meant someone else in general. "Drew can stuff his warm woolly socks where the sun doesn't shine."

"Hang in there," Tina said again, sounding weary. "If you do need money, for a facial mask or anything else, there's some extra cash in a pink box in the bottom drawer of the filing cabinet."

"I don't need your money. I wouldn't want snail goop on my face anyway."

"Me neither. I prefer the natural clay mud they use out here at the spa. You should come here sometime." She paused. "On second thought, maybe don't. Or at least book yourself under a different name."

"Ha ha," Megan said, and they said goodbye.

After the call, Megan went into the office, opened the bottom drawer of the filing cabinet, and checked in the pink box. There was, as Tina promised, a small roll of cash.

There was also a note that read: *Megan, this is for emergency use only, such as for medical emergencies. Do not take it. Love, Tina.*

Megan left the money. She'd only checked the stash out of curiosity.

But the note gave her an idea. The regular rules of the world were allowed to be broken if someone was having an emergency. A medical emergency.

And Megan did know a doctor, so if she *did* happen to have an emergency—such as a catastrophic and painful problem with a tooth—that doctor would have to help her, no matter how much lemon wedge he'd taken in the eye the night before.

On her way out of the flower shop, she grabbed a pair of pliers.

Chapter 13

Back home, Megan Gardenia set the pliers on the bathroom counter along with the phone number for Dr. Drew Morgan's after-hours answering service.

She looked at her teeth in the mirror while Muffins swished around her feet lovingly.

"No chicken tonight," she told him.

He swished her ankles some more. Muffins, like Megan, did not give up easily when there was something he wanted.

Megan ignored the cat and examined each tooth, one by one.

The obvious candidate for a dental emergency was the cap on one of her front teeth. Her natural tooth had been broken years ago by a boy in the neighborhood. The horrible kid had hit her in the face with a rock. Granted, she'd been holding his face in a mud puddle at the time, but nobody deserved a broken tooth. The boy and his family moved away shortly after but not before they paid for the cap on Megan's tooth. It hadn't been cheap.

Megan smiled at herself in the mirror, making a mental note of how the front of her mouth was supposed to look.

She checked the time and used her phone to double-check the regular hours at Drew's clinic. They were open some Saturdays, but they would have been closed for an hour already.

Megan picked up the pliers, grabbed the tooth that had been capped, and pulled. She felt pressure all through the front of her face, and then nothing. The cap had come off with surprising ease.

She leaned over the bathroom counter and gave herself a gap-toothed grin. She resembled a jack-o'-lantern. That called for a selfie! She took a picture on her phone as evidence of her real dental emergency, just in case she was questioned later by the dental authorities.

The front of her mouth ached, and her eyes watered. Her sinuses felt funny.

Megan wondered if yanking off her dental cap with a pair of pliers had been such a great idea. Looking at the sickly little stump that usually lived inside the cap made her feel unclean. Why hadn't she thoroughly brushed her teeth and used mouthwash before attempting home dentistry? Now she needed something to make sure her mouth wasn't too germy. Something stronger than mouthwash.

She went to the fridge, located a bottle of vodka, and brought it back to the bathroom. She poured a splash into the only shot glass in the house—a fiftieth birthday glass someone had given her mother—and tossed it back.

Oops. She'd meant to swoosh the vodka around in her mouth. Better luck next time. She poured another shot, swooshed it around her mouth that time, then gulped. She probably should have spat in the sink, she realized after the fact.

She called the number for Dr. Drew Morgan's answering service.

A familiar male voice said, "Hello?"

It wasn't an answering service. It was Drew, and he'd answered with a hello instead of with a professional greeting.

"Wrong number." She ended the call and set the phone on the counter.

The phone lit up with an incoming call. Megan shrieked.

Muffins, who had been hanging out in the tub, licking the drips from the tap, startled and ripped out of the bathroom in a tumbleweed of cat fur and whiskers.

Megan answered the call with a fake accent. "Allo?"

"Meenie?"

"Me no meanie. You meanie! Wrong number." She didn't end the call. She stayed on the line, holding her breath and waiting to hear his voice.

Drew said, "I know it's you, and I know you're on the line. Why'd you call me?"

"You called me," she said.

"Only because you called me first."

"That was an accident. My phone was in my pocket. It must have been a butt dial. You know how my butt is."

"The last time I saw your butt, it was storming out of O'Hannigan's Pub."

"O'Flannigan's," she said.

"What can I do for you? Are you having a dental emergency? You must be having a dental emergency because this is my special phone number that's only for after-hours emergencies."

She snorted. "I know that. As a matter of fact, I am having a dental emergency."

"Oh." He sounded concerned.

Hearing his softness made her feel extremely light-headed. She chalked it up to the two vodka shots.

"It's my front tooth," she said, pronouncing it *toof*. "Ma toof is broken. The boy down the street broke it."

"Who? When? Did you call the police?"

"It was a long time ago. I have a cap, and it fell off. It fell off ma toof." She was enjoying saying *ma toof* through the hole in the front of her mouth.

"What did your regular dentist say? The one who put the cap on and has all your dental charts?"

"Nothing, because... she died." Megan's dentist was a nice lady who'd been in excellent health at the last checkup.

"Meenie, are you trying to get me over there for a house call?"

"Are you doing anything important? Are you on a date right now?"

He chuckled softly.

Megan pictured Drew's handsome face lit up by a smile. He sounded so appealing. He sounded like he was wearing a cardigan.

"Give me your address," he said.

"Just a minute. Let me get a pen so I can write it down," she said.

Drew laughed. "You don't need a pen. I'm sure you know your own address. What's going on over there? Have you been drinking?"

"Never," she said. "Just a bit. I had to make sure the stump was clean. Ma toof is a stump."

"Give me your address. I'll grab my stuff and make a house call. Meenie?"

"Yeah?"

"Don't throw away the cap. I don't have the equipment in my bag to make a new one. We'll have to adhere that one if it's in good condition, at least temporarily."

She snorted. "I wouldn't throw out ma toof."

She gave him her address, ended the call, and retrieved the tooth cap from the garbage bin where she'd tossed it.

Then she frantically changed clothes and drank another vodka shot before he got there.

When the doorbell rang, she was pulling on the flowered dress she'd worn to a funeral and two weddings. With black socks.

She yanked open the door. "That was fast," she said. "Were you sitting outside my house stalking me?"

"It turns out I don't live that far away."

Drew was wearing a cardigan. It was the color of pumpkin pie. He wore a collared shirt underneath, and his lower half was looking equally respectable in a pair of casual pants.

She looked him over and asked, "Do you even own a pair of jeans?"

"Would you prefer having your tooth fixed by a man in jeans? I could give you a referral."

"You'll do." She waved him in.

He came in, carrying the most adorable leather bag Megan had ever seen. It looked like something a country doctor would bring to deliver a baby in a movie.

Drew wasted no time finding the dining room table, turning the overhead light on to its brightest setting, and then setting out some tools on the table.

She ran to the bathroom, grabbed the cap, tossed the pliers in the laundry hamper, then ran back to Drew and dropped the cap in his palm. He carefully—lovingly, even—set the cap on a shining silver tray on the table.

"Next, a little sterilization," he said as he pulled some bottles from his leather bag. "Take a seat."

She sat in one of the dining room chairs and gave him a magnificent jack-o'-lantern smile. "Gimme back ma toof, doctor."

"Oof," he said. "That's one ugly stump."

She crossed her arms. "You had your tongue right next to my stump last night at O'Flannigan's, and you had no idea what was happening."

"You're right about that. I had no idea what was happening." He cleaned the cap and examined it. "But then I talked to Jim, and we made some sense of it."

"Jim?"

"From the support group. He says you call him Bald Guy Number Two."

"You know people from the support group? Besides me? That's cheating. Feather said we're not supposed to mess with the group dynamic."

"Jim was at the pub last night. He came over after you went off in a huff. He's a pretty cool guy. Did you know he was a fighter pilot? Jim's got some great stories."

"Too bad he never brings up the good stuff in the group. He's always talking about his ex-wife. He's obsessed with her. He visits her every Sunday. Talk about a stalker."

"Jim's wife is dead. He goes to the cemetery and talks to her grave on Sundays." Drew adjusted his rubber gloves and stared at her, his expression neutral.

Megan shivered and rubbed her forearms. "Oh. *That* Jim. I must have been thinking about Bald Guy Number One."

"Do you even listen to the people at your group?" He reached for her face. "Tilt your head back and open up."

She might have answered his question, but he had his hands in her mouth. She could only gurgle in protest. Of course she listened to the people at her group. Why else would she go?

"Jim has some really good insights into women and relationships," Drew said. "Feather gave everyone a reading list, and he's read every book on the list."

Megan made a questioning sound around his gloved hands. What reading list?

"Jim and I had a good talk about boundaries and how important they are for healthy relationships."

She gurgled.

"Boundaries are where you end and other people begin," Drew said. "You know how people talk about drawing the line somewhere? That's about boundaries."

Megan didn't bother responding. She was too busy trying not to choke on her saliva. Drew had brought the basic tools, but the basic tools didn't include a suction tube.

"Hang on," Drew said, sensing her discomfort. "Give it a second while the adhesive sets up. Thank you in advance for not biting me."

The scent of the adhesive made her eyes water. A tear slipped down one cheek. Drew either didn't notice or chose not to comment.

"If you and I are going to keep dating, we're going to have to set some boundaries," Drew said. "I draw the line at you storming off without any explanation. I know I'm not perfect, but it's not fair to me if you don't tell me what I'm doing wrong. How am I supposed to grow as a person if I don't get told about my flaws?"

She gave him a helpless look, and not just because his hands were still in her mouth. How was she supposed to tell Drew his flaws when that was what she always did to guys, and it always drove them away?

Finally, he released her mouth. "All done," he said. "No more jack-o'-lantern face."

She wiped her cheek. "That glue made my eyes water," she said.

"I'm glad it was just the glue." He pulled down the medical mask that had been covering his mouth. His smile was so tender, it almost made her cry for real.

"That's it?" She ran her tongue over the stumpy spot and found only a tooth. "That was fast."

"How does it feel?"

She flicked the spot with her tongue again. "You put it on backwards."

He frowned, which she found adorable.

He thrust his hands at her jaw. "Let me see it." He sounded annoyed, which she also enjoyed.

"Wait," she said, turning her face away. "It's not backwards. I was testing your boundaries."

"You do that a lot," he said.

"What about you? Coming over here, with your cardigan and your mask and your caring eyes. You're going to give me a dentist fetish. My next visit for a checkup at my usual dentist is going to be awkward."

"I thought your dentist died?"

"Did I say that?"

He slowly took off his gloves. "I should get going," he said. "How did you get that cap off anyway? Pliers?"

"I bit into a hard apple."

"Meenie, I can take a little teasing, but Jim says one of the most important boundaries is that we're always completely honest with each other."

"Sounds like you should be dating Jim."

"We're going fishing tomorrow."

"Feather might not like that."

"I'll deal with Feather." He gave her a serious look. "Did you hear what I said about boundaries?"

She sat up straight in her chair. "I pulled off the cap with a pair of pliers because I needed an excuse to call you. When Luca broke his leg, it was what got him back together with my sister. When there's a medical emergency, all the regular rules go out the window."

"You didn't need an excuse to call me," he said gently. "Please don't put anything in your mouth but food."

"No more using my molars to open beer bottles?"

Drew shuddered visibly.

"What about tongues?" She smoothed down her dress and gave him a coy, non-jack-o'-lantern look. "Not mine but other people's tongues, in general?"

"That should be fine," he said, but he didn't lean in for a kiss. "What happened last night at the pub?"

"I thought you wanted to sleep with me."

"Is that so wrong of me? What's wrong with you? Do you lose all respect for a guy when he shows interest in you? Is it like that Oscar Wilde saying that he wouldn't want to be a member in any club that would have him?"

His words flooded over her. Only a third of what he was saying made any sense. Her adrenaline was riding high, and the vodka was blotting out crucial parts of her critical-thinking facilities.

"Shut up and kiss me," she said.

"I shouldn't," he said. "Jim told me not to."

"I'm going to kill Jim."

"He means well. He's been through a lot."

"Are we going to talk about Jim all night, or are you going to help me take this tooth for a test ride?"

He took off the face mask, put everything away, snapped his medical bag shut, and set it aside.

"Your tooth should be secure," he said.

"It feels wiggly."

"No it doesn't."

"How would you know?"

Drew shook his head and gave her a look that said he knew he shouldn't kiss her.

Then he leaned forward, and he did it anyway.

Chapter 14

Sunday

Rory Taylor showed up at the usual time Sunday morning to do laundry at the Gardenia family's main house.

Rory usually did her laundry with Tina while Megan did some baking, but Tina was still away with Luca, so Rory was stuck with Megan.

"I don't want to impose," Rory said, hesitating in the doorway. "If you don't want me around, I understand. I mean, Tina's not here."

"You're my friend too," Megan said. "And this is practically your house. You grew up here, just like I did. That's why we always say you're the undocumented third sister. Now get in here and hand over those donuts."

Rory came in, and Megan dashed around the house, grabbing her clothes. She joined Rory in the laundry room for sorting.

When it came to laundry day with Rory, a person had to follow the rules. The first load was always Rory's underwear, which Rory had to throw directly into the machine straight from an opaque bag with nobody looking.

That Sunday, she did so then topped the load with other clothes and set it to wash. Rory didn't mind either Gardenia sister seeing her clothes after they'd been washed.

Megan dumped out the laundry hamper from the bathroom. The pliers fell to the floor with a clunk. Megan let out a guilty laugh.

Rory looked at the pliers then at Megan. "What's that all about?"

"Funny story," Megan said. "I used those pliers to pull off my dental cap so I could call Drew. He's a dentist, and he makes house calls."

"He came over here? Last night?"

"He did. He glued my tooth on, and then he glued himself to me." Megan waved a hand. "Vodka was involved."

Rory swallowed hard. "You guys seem to have a lot of chemistry," she said.

"You think?" Megan fanned her face. Was she blushing?

"I'm happy for you. Was it the same guy I met on Friday night? I'm confused. Teenie told me you guys had some sort of argument that night."

"We made up," Megan said. "It was a good make up."

Rory kept her eyes on her laundry.

"Drew's got a fever, and I'm the cure," Megan said. "Last night was hot."

Rory covered her ears and gave Megan a hurt look.

Megan said, "It's all out of my system now, Rory. I won't say anything else."

Rory pushed around her remaining piles, which were mostly black pants and skirts from her catering job.

"We can talk about relationships if you want," Rory said. "Just not the physical stuff."

"Then there's not much left to tell you about last night because things got very physical. I might have left some bruises on the poor guy. I don't know for sure because he snuck out in the middle of the night, so I didn't get a good look at him in the light of day."

Rory nodded, took a few breaths, then she said, "I saw Howard yesterday."

"My ex?" There weren't a lot of guys their age named Howard, so Megan knew exactly who Rory meant.

"I saw him at work," Rory said. "We're catering his engagement dinner."

"Howard's getting married?" The news hurt, but Megan shook it off. "Good for him. How'd he pull that off? Did his parents pay for one of those mail-order brides?"

"His fiancée is local, and she sounds nice," Rory said. She bit her lip, like she was on the verge of revealing something.

Megan said, "And? Spit it out."

"Howard's a nice guy, Meenie. He told me some of the things you said to him when you were breaking up. They were pretty bad. You shouldn't talk to people like that."

"He started it. He's the one who broke up with me."

"But why couldn't you let it go?" Rory looked genuinely curious. "I don't get it. You grew up with a nice, normal family."

"My family wasn't exactly normal."

"Sure, but it wasn't like mine."

"Rory, I wish you'd shut up about how bad you had it growing up. Maybe some of us are just born screwed up. Have you ever thought about that? You blame your family for how you are, but maybe you just came out that way, already wired to be screwed up. Everybody feels sorry for you, and we all bend over backward to accommodate your little quirks, but nobody ever feels bad for me."

Softly, Rory said, "I feel bad for you."

"Well, you shouldn't. My life is awesome. I'd appreciate it if you didn't go talking to Howard behind my back."

Rory stopped the washing machine and pulled out her clothes, which were sopping wet. She started stuffing them into her bag.

"Don't go," Megan said.

"You're being mean."

"It's my boundaries. My boundaries make me say stuff I shouldn't."

"That's not how boundaries work."

"You got me. I haven't read any of the books people keep telling me to read."

"Of course you haven't." Rory continued stuffing the sopping-wet laundry into her bag.

Megan said, "Why do I need to read a bunch of books? Why can't I be around people who accept me for who I am?"

"Because you're mean," Rory said. "It's not an attractive quality in a person."

"That's not what Dr. Drew Morgan said last night. He likes me how I am."

"He was probably drunk off the vodka fumes coming off of your breath. How much did you drink? I can still smell it all over you."

"You do not."

"I do."

"Maybe you should go." Megan plunged her hands into the washing machine and started helping Rory pull out the sopping-wet clothes.

When it was unloaded, Rory hoisted the heavy bag on her shoulder and walked out, dripping the whole way.

"Great chat!" Megan yelled after her. "Always a pleasure, Rory!"

In another minute or two, Megan might have chased Rory outside and convinced her to come back.

She might even have apologized, but she was interrupted by an alert on her phone.

A text message came in from Drew.

Drew: Did you have a good sleep?

Megan: Why did you leave before I woke up? I didn't even get to make you my famous full English breakfast.

Drew: It's complicated. I had to get up early to go fishing with Jim.

Megan: Are you with Jim right now? Are you two actually fishing, like a couple of old men? Send a photo.

Drew: I don't want to talk about it like this, over text.

Megan: Talk about what?

Drew: Things got out of hand last night. I shouldn't have been drinking.

Megan: I wasn't pouring the vodka down your throat. You wanted it.

Drew: I wanted something.

Megan: What's that supposed to mean?

Drew: I'm not going to visit the support group anymore. You can go on Tuesday.

Megan: Are you breaking up with me?

There was a long, awful pause, and then a longer text came back.

Drew: If that's what you want to call it, sure. You're a great person, but I don't think I have what you need right now.

Megan: Did Jim make you say that? Is he making you write these messages? You need to push him off the boat and drown him so he can be with his dead wife.

Drew: That's not very nice.

Megan composed a few different messages but couldn't find the right combination of emojis to express how she felt.

Finally, she sent a single skull then switched off her phone.

Chapter 15

Monday

On Monday, Drew didn't call or text.

Megan Gardenia yelled at a longtime customer and earned the flower shop a bad review online.

Chapter 16

Tuesday

On Tuesday, big sister Tina Gardenia fixed the "misunderstanding" with the unhappy customer from the previous day. The customer changed the review from bad to good, raving about Tina, the "best florist in town."

Tina also smoothed things over with Rory, who said she shouldn't have brought up Howard with Megan, and that the argument wasn't *entirely* Megan's fault.

Tina gently suggested that Megan attend the self-help group that night, or take the money from the pink box and pay to see Feather for some one-on-one counseling.

Megan did not take the suggestion well.

At ten minutes to eight on Tuesday night, ten minutes before the group session would be starting, Megan, who was at home sulking, decided she would go to group therapy after all.

Feather had given Megan the choice of dating Drew or coming to the group, and since the first option wasn't happening, Megan had no choice but to go.

Mostly for the good of the group. The group needed her there, of course.

Chapter 17

Megan tried to sneak into the group session quietly, but the squeaky door gave her away. Feather turned around. A look of disappointment crossed the blond therapist's face but quickly disappeared in a professional smile. She gestured for Megan to come in and take a seat.

The gang was all there, all watching her.

Jim was there too. Jim, a.k.a. Bald Guy Number Two, a.k.a. the guy who'd been meddling with Drew's head, first at O'Flannigan's then on his fishing boat.

Megan glared at Jim. Why couldn't he get over his dead wife and leave other people alone?

"Carla was telling us about Max," Feather said. "Go ahead, Carla."

Carla said, "Today is the one-year anniversary of Max's death. I went by the dog bakery where I used to buy his favorite treats, and I… I saw something."

The group leaned in, interested.

"There was a poster on the bulletin board," Carla said. "For German Shepherd puppies."

Everyone went, "Awww."

Feather asked, "Do you think you might be ready to bring a new pet into your life?"

"Oh no." Carla shook her head. "Puppies are a lot of work. They need to be trained, and I'm not as young as I used to be."

"What about an older dog?" Feather asked.

Carla said, "Nobody could replace Max."

"Of course not," Feather said. "But the love you feel for another dog would be in a different place in your heart."

"I'm not sure about that," the librarian said. "Isn't all love the same? Love is love."

Ryan said, "Love is love, but there are different kinds."

Megan thought about Muffins, and how she would never love another cat the way she did him. But cats were cats, and they didn't know to be jealous of some other cat you used to have.

For the next hour, Megan thought about types of love.

She also glared at Jim, who avoided eye contact.

Feather made some general observations then read aloud from a book about boundaries that she was recommending to the whole group.

Feather asked, "Does anyone else have any book recommendations.

Megan's hand shot up.

Feather said, "I mean books about relationships."

Megan waved her hand frantically.

Feather gestured for her to speak.

Megan said, "I've been reading a book in the bathroom. I have an old copy of *The Secret Rules of Love* that my mom picked up at a garage sale." *The Secret Rules of Love* was a popular book that had come out in the nineties and was widely criticized by every female journalist who wouldn't admit she owned a copy and had used it to catch a husband.

Feather said, "And? Did you learn anything?"

"No," Megan said, snorting. "But if you want a report, I'll give you one. It's a book written by two train wreck ladies with no professional credentials between them, and it's all about tricking guys into thinking women are a prize to be won. It's total garbage."

Jim said, "That's not garbage. A good woman is a prize to be cherished."

Some of the ladies nodded in agreement.

Megan glared at Jim until her eyes hurt. "Shut up, Jim," she said. "You weren't that good to your wife back when she was still alive, and we all know it."

There was a collective gasp around the group. Everyone knew it was true. Jim always talked about his regrets, and how he'd drank too much and yelled too much when his wife had been around.

Jim's eyes glistened. He said, "And those are my greatest regrets in life."

Feather said, "Megan, we don't tell people to shut up. You need to apologize to Jim."

"I had that coming," Jim said. "I have a confession to make to everyone. I'm afraid I did something over the weekend that might have upset Meenie."

The group murmured with interest.

Feather asked, "Is it something appropriate for sharing with the group?"

"I talked to the new guy," Jim said. "The good-lookin' fellow in the suit. Did you know he's a dentist?"

"I knew that," Megan said.

Abbie leaned over and whispered to Megan, "A dentist is practically a doctor. That's a good catch, dear."

Jim said, "Drew and I went fishing."

Megan pointed her finger at Jim's bald head. "You stole him from me." She explained to the group, "Drew went fishing with Jim, and Jim brainwashed him into sending me a message saying he despised me."

Feather asked, "Who sent the message? That doesn't sound like the Jim we know."

Jim held both hands up. "I didn't tell the boy what to say. He did that on his own." He gave Megan a sad look. "You might not believe me, but I tried to talk him into giving you another shot." He looked over at Feather. "I think I accidentally did reverse psychology on the boy. He did the opposite of what I suggested."

"That happens," Feather said. "It happens a lot, actually."

Carla waved her hand. "Did I miss a meeting? I could have sworn I was here last week. What happened with Drew and Meenie? I liked him. He was cute. He reminded me of my Max."

The librarian told Carla, "They went on a date at O'Flannigan's Pub on Friday. There was another girl there at first, then she left. Drew and Meenie kissed each other, right in public at the table where everyone could see them, then she threw a glass of wine in his face and stormed out."

"It was only water," Megan said. "Not wine. And how did you know? Did Jim tell you, or have all of you guys been spying on me?"

The librarian straightened up and folded her hands on her laps daintily. "I was there having a white wine spritzer with a friend."

"What a coincidence," Megan said, turning to glare at Bald Guy Number Two. "Jim was there too. Are you two dirty birds secretly knocking boots?"

Ryan, the man with the moving-surface phobias, said, "It's not exactly a secret. We've all seen the way you two make googly eyes with each other."

Abbie said, "I didn't know."

Carla said, "I must have missed some meetings."

Bald Guy Number One asked, "Is everybody here hooking up with everybody else?"

Around the circle, people giggled.

Feather said, "That's enough about that. Let's get back to book recommendations."

Megan shot the therapist a furious look. "Is that all you're going to say to them? Jim and the librarian are hooking up, and you're just going to let them do that and keep coming to the group, making googly eyes at each other?"

"They're both adults," Feather said.

"I have a name," the librarian said.

Ryan said to Megan, "I've only hooked up with someone from the group one time. She doesn't come to meetings anymore, so it won't be a problem if you ever want to take me out for a drink. You can throw a drink in my face any time."

"Ew," Megan said. "You're not ugly or anything, but I couldn't be with a guy who's afraid of escalators. What if you were on top of me and I moved, which is something I do, and you locked up?"

Ryan grinned. "I'm not ugly?"

"You're kinda cute," she said. "Okay. You're attractive. To be honest, I only came to this group because I thought it was for weight loss, but I thought you were interesting, so I came back the next week. But then you told us your story, and I found out you didn't have the man parts I'm looking for in a guy."

Someone asked, "Ryan doesn't have man parts? Does she mean he's…"

"I have man parts," Ryan said. "But I get what you're saying," he said to Megan. "It's hard for a woman to respect a guy who can't bring home the bacon because he's too terrified of the grocery store."

Feather said, "We all have our flaws. If our loved ones were perfect, they might not choose to be around flawed people such as us."

The librarian said, "That's easy for you to say because you're perfect."

Before Feather could speak, Megan said, "Feather's *not* perfect. She just looks that way. She's got some bad ideas. She thought Drew and I should date each other one-on-one instead of coming to the group. It wasn't a good idea. It didn't even last a week."

Abbie patted Megan on the shoulder. "At least you tried. Don't worry, dear. So what if Drew wasn't the one for you? There are plenty of fish in the sea."

Ryan said, brightly, "Last week I found a convenience store near my house with no conveyer belts."

Megan waved her hands in frustration. "Ryan, why don't you just stop wearing scarves? Huh? If you're not wearing scarves, you won't have anything to worry about getting caught in moving surfaces."

The group was silent. Everyone had been thinking it, but nobody had dared say it until now.

Ryan reached protectively for the scarf he always wore, even in warm weather. "But then people would see my neck when I'm outside."

"You're hopeless," Megan said. "But let's make a deal. If you can go two weeks without wearing the scarf, I'll take you out for a drink. I may or may not throw one in your face."

"Hmm," he said, appearing to mull it over.

Feather said, "I believe we may be making some real progress here tonight. Is anyone else feeling uncomfortable? Sometimes that's a good sign."

Abbie put her arm around Megan. "I like it when Meenie tells us what she thinks. No offense, Feather, I appreciate your advice, but I wish you'd come right out and tell us what you're thinking sometimes. Everyone's always so worried about people getting offended that they don't dare speak up. It's good for the group to have someone like Meenie because she's the only one who calls us out on our stupidity."

Megan turned to Abbie and said, "Tell your sister you're done putting up with her whining. Call it what it is: whining. And when you two go for lunch at one of those fancy overpriced places she insists on dragging you to, make her pay for it. If she's got such a bad memory, just tell her you paid last time, and it's her turn."

Feather made a sound of disagreement but didn't speak.

Jim said, "Actually, that's good advice. You should try it, Abbie."

Ryan raised his hand and asked Megan, "What's the difference between sharing your feelings and whining?"

"Sharing your feelings is kind of boring, but I guess some of it has to slip out," Megan said. "Whining is when you never do anything about it."

The group shifted uncomfortably in their chairs. A couple of people muttered that there had been a lot of whining lately.

"New rule," Megan said confidently. "No more whining."

The group was still and silent, frozen by the magnificence of Megan's idea.

Feather sighed wearily.

"Let's take a vote," Megan said. "All in favor of making a rule for no more whining, raise your hands."

Everyone put up a hand.

Slowly, reluctantly, the group's leader and coach, Feather, put hers up as well. "Why not," she said.

"Good," Megan said, feeling very satisfied. "I'm not going to whine about my dating life. Drew wasn't the guy for me. The problem wasn't me. It was him. Dentists must be very picky. Delusional, even. They call themselves doctors when they aren't really full doctors. Who does that? Anyway, there's no need to discuss it further because that would just be *whining*."

Feather said, "I wouldn't go so far as to…" Her face went pale, and her hand went to her mouth. She was having another round of pregnancy nausea. She pushed her chair back and stood. "Excuse me for a few minutes. Please carry on as you were."

Feather left, and they did carry on.

They didn't get through everyone's issues that night, but they did make some really good progress, as far as Megan was concerned.

She even told Jim and the librarian they could keep knocking boots as long as they shared some juicy stuff with the group each week.

Chapter 18

Wednesday

Howard Hamilton didn't want to see Megan Gardenia, which was why she had to book an appointment with him under a fake name.

When she walked into the accountant's office, Howard looked up from his computer and said, "Oh no. It's you."

"Way to make a potential client feel welcome." She plopped into the guest chair on the other side of Howard's large, paperwork-covered desk.

"You're not a potential client," he said grimly. "You're an existing one we can't get rid of."

"I don't trust anyone else with Gardenia Flowers' bookkeeping," Megan said. "You're the only person I know who's anal-retentive enough to keep track of all our taxes and submission deadlines. You're an invaluable member of our corporate team. I've asked around the city, and nobody's as anal as you."

Howard squinted behind his thick glasses. "I know there's a compliment in there somewhere."

"I hear you're getting married," she said. "We're doing the flowers, I'm sure."

"You're not," he said.

"I'll talk to your fiancée. What's her name?"

"No way." Howard shook his head. "I'm not letting you poison anything else in my life. It's bad enough I have to deal with you at tax season."

Megan laughed. "You're so funny. I miss this. We used to have fun together, Howie-doodles."

He took a breath high in his chest and deflated. "What can I do for you today? My assistant booked you for a full hour. I'll give you ten minutes, but only if you don't mention anything below my belt."

"Oh, Howie-doodles. Don't get your lady knickers in a twist."

"That's it." He stood and pointed to the door. "Get out."

"Okay, okay," she said. "I'll keep it above the belt. Speaking of which, did you ever find out if the doctors could do anything about your pepperoni nipples?"

"Please leave," he said, still pointing.

"Not before you tell me something I need to know. I'm doing a research project."

He sighed again as he sat back down.

Howard was a highly intelligent and resourceful man, but he knew he wasn't as strong as Megan physically. He knew he wouldn't be able to kick her out of his office, not even with the help of his assistant, who should have known better than to book a one-hour appointment with a woman who called herself Hilda Horsetrousers.

"You can have one question," he said.

"That's all I need. I can be quick, like you. I can be in and out in under two minutes."

Howard's nostrils flared. He waved for her to ask her question.

"I've been wondering about the difference between girls who are the marrying kind and girls who aren't. Rather than whining about it, I figured I should go straight to the horse's mouth and ask guys who are getting married, like you. When you met your fiancée, how did you know she was the marrying type?"

Howard's frown eased for the first time since Megan had walked in. His face settled into a smile but not a particularly nice one.

Speaking slowly, as though savoring the moment, he said, "That's easy. When I met my fiancée, I knew she was the one because she was the exact opposite of you."

"No more joking around, Howie-doodles. Tell me for real."

"I'm not joking around."

"Don't even try. You're not good at it," Megan said.

"I'll prove it." He pressed the intercom button for his assistant. "Dana, can you tell me what it was, exactly, that I said about Charlotte after I took her on our first date?"

Dana replied over the intercom, "You said she was beautiful. Why does Hilda Horsetrousers need to know about that?" Dana was new and didn't know who Megan was.

Howard's malicious smile faded slightly.

"I knew it," Megan said, jabbing the air with her finger. "All you could talk about was her looks. Guys are so shallow."

Howard waved for her to calm down. He spoke into the intercom calmly. "And there was something else, Dana. Something about her personality."

"Oh!" Dana sounded excited. "You said Charlotte was exactly who you'd been praying for. You said that God must have heard your prayers and answered because Charlotte was the exact opposite of that horrible girl from the flower shop. Megan. The one who was so mean."

Howard's malicious smile went to maximum. "Thank you, Dana." He released the intercom button.

"You set this up," Megan said, getting to her feet. "You knew it was me coming in, and you set this whole thing up to get back at me."

"I did not," Howard said. "That would be crazy."

"*You're* crazy," she said, and she left without another word.

Howard hadn't been any help at all, but Megan was moving forward.

She certainly wasn't going to keep going over and over events of the past and talking about it with people, like some sort of whiner.

Chapter 19

Friday

After a long week of making bouquets for brides with fall weddings and making no progress figuring out what those lucky women had that Megan didn't, Megan took herself out for a date on Friday night.

First, she took herself to dinner at Delilah's for a sausage pizza

then to a movie at the local neighborhood theater. It was the popular one with the superheroes. It was okay.

After the movie, she took herself to O'Flannigan's for a drink.

Unfortunately, the pub was already too busy by the time the movie ended, and she didn't see a free table.

Megan was heading back out of the pub when someone tapped her shoulder from behind. When she turned, nobody was there. She turned the other way and saw Drew, grinning from the childish trick.

"Oh. It's just you," she said.

"You're not leaving already, are you?"

She was confused by his friendly tone. They hadn't spoken since she'd sent him the emoji that indicated he was dead to her.

"It's too busy in here," she said. "I couldn't find a seat."

"Come in and sit with me and the guys."

"The guys from the support group? Is Jim here?"

"No. I mean, I don't know. He might be around here. I meant the guys I used to play rugby with. I didn't know it, but they meet here all the time. I'm glad you brought me here and got me back in touch with them."

"I'm glad something good came of our regrettable time together."

Drew looked wounded by her words. "Regrettable? I had a great time with you. Why haven't you returned my messages? I figured we could hang out sometimes, maybe take it slow. Can't we be friends?"

"After you sent me those *lovely* texts from the warm embrace of Jim and his fishing boat, I've been too busy to read whatever else you sent." She hadn't been too busy to delete every message seconds after arrival. "We've had a lot of fall weddings this year. It's like marriage fever for some people."

"How about you? How have you been?"

There was movement behind Drew that caught her eye. Megan noticed a group of guys at a nearby table, all looking at them with interest rather than watching one of the many large-screen televisions.

Megan observed the guys then turned back to Drew, her eyes narrowed with suspicion.

"I see what you're doing," Megan said. "All your little buddies are over there, watching you, and you want to keep me talking to you as long as possible so they can have a good look at your last conquest. You're a real champion, Drew."

She turned and shoved her way through the crowd until she was outside. She stuffed her hands in her hoodie pockets and started walking home.

There were footfalls behind her—men's dress shoes on pavement—and Drew caught up with her, breathing heavily.

"That wasn't what I was doing," he said. "Not exactly. I told them about you but only because I wanted a second opinion. I wasn't making fun of you, and I wasn't bragging."

"You should have bragged about bagging me," she said. "I'm a real catch."

"Slow down," he said, breathing heavily.

"Get more regular exercise," she said, pretending she wasn't breathing hard from the pace too.

"Fine. I'll walk you home," he said.

"It's a free country."

They crossed a street, and she slowed her pace to something she could keep up all the way home.

He asked, "How's the group, anyway? Did you go on Tuesday?"

"Yes. They all want to know why you abandoned them, Drew. How could you do that to a bunch of people who are all basket cases with abandonment issues on top of their other weird phobias?"

"I should come back next Tuesday and apologize."

"I'm sure your boyfriend Jim would love that. Be careful. I bet he's planning a threesome for you and the librarian."

"Thanks for the warning," he said. "You're really mad at me, aren't you?"

"This is just how my face looks."

"That night when you were pouring the vodka shots, you said you were happy with us just keeping it casual for a while. It's not fair that you're mad at me for doing exactly what you wanted."

"Haven't you figured out that girls don't tell you what they want?"

"Are you talking about you or all girls? Because no, I haven't noticed that. Not with anyone but you. I guess that's why you're so complicated."

She snorted. "Back in the nineteen forties, complicated women like me used to get lobotomies."

"You're not mentally ill, Meenie. You're just difficult."

"How do you know I'm not mentally ill? We did meet at a therapy group."

He chuckled. "Did I ever tell you why I showed up there?"

"Because you had a two-year dry spell, and you wanted to break the spell by picking up someone with low self-esteem. Did you know Jim and the librarian are making the beast with two backs? That group is a hotbed of sexual activity. And most of them are *so old*. I wonder if Pfizer is secretly sponsoring the group to sell more little blue pills."

"Don't you want to know why I really showed up?"

"Because you looked through the window in the door, and you saw me." She stopped walking and grabbed him by the shoulders. "How romantic. It was love at first sight." She tilted her head back and closed her eyes. "Take me now, you romantic beast. I cannot live without your stuff touching my stuff in the dark."

"Don't tempt me," he said, his voice sounding husky. "I walked in that night because I didn't read the card on the door. I thought it was a group for investments."

Megan straightened her head and opened her eyes. "Are you lying to me?"

He shook his head. "Honestly, I thought it was a meeting about investments. The woman who does investment consultations runs a session up the hall, and her name—"

"Is Heather," Megan finished. "Heather with an H." She blinked at Drew. "That checks out," she said.

"I figured out pretty quickly it wasn't a group for investing, but then I stayed because of…" He leaned in until their faces were very close. "Jim," he whispered. "The way the light reflects off his bald head drives me wild. You should have seen him when we were fishing."

Megan felt the heat in her body rising from Drew's proximity. "I knew it," she whispered back. "You'll have to share him with the librarian."

"I'm into her too."

"Now that I've broken your dry spell, I've turned you into a sex addict," she said. "I'll have to refer you down the hall to the sex addict recovery group. I'll warn you, though. They're not as good-looking as our group of randos."

"Did you say *our* group?"

"Mine and Jim's," she said.

"Jim," he whispered, and he closed in for the kiss.

Chapter 20

Saturday

Megan Gardenia woke up with two guys in her bed. One of them was Muffins, who was lying on Megan's chest and giving her a judgmental stare.

"Be nice," she told the cat.

He flicked his tail then jumped off the bed and trotted out of the room. Clearly *someone* didn't approve of Megan having a friend stay over.

Megan called after the cat, "Don't you dare put a dead mouse in Drew's shoes."

Drew rolled over to face Megan. "What did you just say about a dead mouse?"

"Don't worry your pretty little head. Muffins doesn't catch a lot of mice anyway. I'm sure your shoes are safe."

"I can't tell if you're joking. Should I be concerned?"

She shook her head. "I'm pretty sure Muffins is *not* putting a rodent carcass in your nice Italian loafers right now. But you should probably give them a shake before you put them on." She ran her fingers over Drew's chest. "I see you forgot to sneak out in the middle of the night this time."

"I didn't sneak out that other time. I had to go on a fishing trip."

"Right," she said. "With your boyfriend, Jim."

"Enough about Jim. Any further talk about Jim is going to lead to things I'm not sure I have the energy for." Drew winced. "My back hurts. What did you do to me in your front yard? One minute I was standing, then I was flat on my back in the grass."

"I swept the leg," she said matter-of-factly.

"But why?"

"Why not? It's the fastest way to get someone to the ground."

"But we were standing on your lawn."

"Exactly. We were on nice, soft grass. I would have wrestled you sooner, but it's not safe on the pavement."

"Do you always wrestle with guys?"

"Just the ones I like." She tapped him on the nose. "Boop."

He tapped her right back. "Boop."

She asked, "Now that I've taught you to watch out for the leg sweep, what else can I do for you? Breakfast in bed? Pack you a bagged lunch for work today?"

He checked the time on her alarm clock. "It's Saturday, which is a light day, but I do have a few patients after lunch."

"What do you mean it's a light day? You're not fully booked? You must not be a very good dentist. Maybe I should get a second opinion on that cap you glued into my mouth all willy-nilly."

He dropped his jaw in mock outrage. "Not a very good dentist? Those are fighting words, you bad girl."

She raised her eyebrows. "Want to take this back out to the front lawn?"

"I think we gave your neighbors enough of a show last night."

"True," she said. "Plus, we already got grass stains all over one change of clothes."

He wrinkled his nose. "Grass stains." He groaned.

He leaned back, resting his head on Megan's second pillow, where Muffins normally slept. The sea-foam-green linens were a perfect complement to his skin tone. His brown eyes were a rich chocolate with bright flecks and an inner ring that was nearly green. The sheets had been purchased to complement Muffins, with his orange fur and entirely green eyes, but they looked even better around Dr. Drew Morgan.

Drew asked, "What are you thinking about?" He reached up to run his fingers through her tangled morning hair. She normally hated that, but it felt good when Drew did it.

"I'm thinking that you look really good in my sheets. You look good in sea-foam green."

"Thanks." He grinned. "I can't wait to see how you look in my bed."

"You think you're going to get me into your bed?"

"Sure. I know how it's done. You just *sweep the leg*."

"I shouldn't have told you all my secrets."

Muffins returned and situated himself between them for a bath.

Drew propped himself up on one elbow and petted the cat. "So what do I have to do to get you to my place in the first place?"

"Reverse psychology works well on me. You could tell me to never come over. You could ban me from your house."

He chuckled. "Whatever you do, *don't* show up naked under a trench coat."

"What makes you think I'd show up naked in a trench coat?"

"You're a wild girl. Exactly what I need right now."

"You need me? Are we talking about, like, a medical type of emergency?"

"You tell me." He scooped up Muffins, placed him on the chair next to the bed, and pulled Megan close to him.

Chapter 21

While Drew took a shower, Megan gathered up their grass-stained clothes.

In the laundry room, she tossed everything into the washing machine. She did not use prewash nor did she presoak any of the stains.

She was in the kitchen when Drew came in wearing a pair of her sweatpants with a white T-shirt.

"Two sizes too small," she said, whistling. "Just how I like my clothes on a man."

"Where are my clothes?"

"In the wash."

"Did you treat the grass stains with prewash?"

She laughed and pretended she knew what he meant. "Sure did. And now I'm making you breakfast." Megan still didn't know what qualities made a girl the marrying kind, but she figured making meals for the guy had to be involved, and she could handle that. Her cooking and baking skills were ten times better than Tina's.

Drew stepped up behind her at the sink and nuzzled her neck. "Let's make breakfast together."

She pushed her neck and shoulder together to squeeze him away gently. His touch was way too intimate.

He pulled away with a chuckle. "Tell me where the coffee stuff is."

"Luca keeps his stuff in here." She opened a cupboard.

"Luca?"

"My sister's boyfriend. I told you about him, didn't I?"

"Motorcycle guy. I remember."

Drew got to work brewing coffee, measuring out the coffee grounds and water meticulously like a high school chemistry teacher making his first batch of crystal meth.

After breakfast, they sat together in the breakfast nook. The large window faced the backyard, and the birds were having a great time at the bird feeder.

"My sister lives over there," Megan said, flicking her chin at the converted garage that was now a cottage. "She's one year older than me and prettier, but she's got a boyfriend now, so don't even think about trading up."

"I wouldn't dream of it."

"You can only have one Gardenia sister. Those are the rules, and they've been the rules since the beginning of time, or at least since I turned twelve and started noticing boys were for more than fighting with."

"Speaking of rules…" He dropped on the table the dog-eared copy of *The Secret Rules of Love* that she'd been leafing through recently—entirely for comedic value. "This is quite the reading material."

"Where'd you find that? Were you digging through my drawers? Whatever you found in there is between me and the company that sends me stuff in plain brown wrappers."

"I wasn't snooping," he said. "It was lying out in the open, in the bathroom."

"We keep that around as a joke," she said. "My mom and my aunt, Jane, think it's hilarious."

He opened it up and read a sentence out loud.

Megan yanked the book from his hand. "You're getting me all worked up. Want to learn a few more wrestling moves?"

"I'd love to, but I really do have to check in at the office. Any chance my clothes are done washing? Maybe you could give me a few pointers while they're in the dryer."

"Game on." Megan jumped up and ran to the laundry room. The washer dinged as she walked in the room.

Drew, who'd followed her in, said, "This is a great old house. When did you say your mother was coming back?"

Megan opened the washing machine and dug out the clothes.

"She might never come back. The woman just *loves* Europe, apparently."

"Do you miss her? My parents live ten blocks away from me. I can't imagine them being out of town for so long. They—" He stopped talking and pulled his tan-colored pants from her hands. "Uh-oh. The grass stains on the knees didn't wash out. Did you pretreat them?"

"Of course I did."

"Did you let the stuff sit on the stains for twenty minutes before you put the clothes in the wash?"

"Not exactly," she said. "Don't worry. I'll run them through the wash again with double soap and bleach."

Drew nudged her out of the way and pulled the other wet clothes back out of the dryer. "What's going on here? These are all different colors. Don't you sort by colors?"

"Calm down, dude. There's nothing bright red in there. I'm not a complete idiot."

He pulled out his shirt and scowled at it. "There's a grass stain on the elbow. You can't dry this. The stain will set."

"Nobody looks at elbows," she said.

"Don't get defensive. I'm not mad at you. I just don't want to stroll into work late with grass stains on my clothes. It's my business. I have to set the tone."

Megan stomped her foot. "I thought it would come out in the wash," she said.

He kissed her forehead. "Don't worry about it. I can buy new clothes. But I am running out of time. Do you mind if I borrow these sweats? I'll swing by my house on the way to work. I might be able to make it, except…" He slapped his forehead. "I walked here last night. My car is parked back at O'Flannigan's."

"You'd better get going. Don't you dare walk out of here with my favorite sweatpants. I might never get them back, knowing how you are with your come-here, go-away antics."

"Me?" He looked down. "Fine. I guess I had that coming."

Megan took his hand. "My mother's got some extra guy clothes in her room."

They went to Lois Gardenia's room, where Megan opened the second unused closet. "This stuff is not as nice as what you usually wear, but it should fit, and it's not grass-stained." She held out a shirt, sea-foam green.

"I do like that color," he said.

Megan shrugged. "The guy had good taste." She tossed some more dress shirts and trousers on the bed.

"I almost hate to ask, but why would someone leave so many clothes behind? These aren't brand-new, but they're nice. Do they belong to your mom's boyfriend?"

"My mother's boyfriend lives in Europe. He's an Italian guy or maybe a Jamaican guy. I've lost track."

She held one of the light-brown shirts up to Drew's neck. It looked right, but she couldn't imagine any color looking bad on Drew.

He took the shirt from her hands. "Whose clothes are these?" he asked.

"Does it matter?"

"Of course it does. That's why I'm asking."

She turned away so he couldn't see her face. It had been stupid of her to bring him in there. She should have figured out how to get the grass stains out of his clothes. Or she should have not wrestled him on the lawn in the first place. She was always so stupid and impulsive and impatient. She did everything wrong.

"Talk to me," he said. "I'm not leaving this room until you do."

"Just get dressed and go. You can't be late for work. You have an important job. People are waiting for you. Patients. You don't have time for me and my dumb stuff."

"I'll call my staff. They can reschedule today's appointments, or one of the other partners can take over for me. I left here too soon once, and I'm not making that mistake again."

She turned around and gave him a sultry look. "You want more of this?"

Drew's face was serious, his brown eyes full of concern. "Talk to me. For real. Feather did say we might be able to help each other."

"I can help you out of those tight sweatpants, if you stop talking." She came at him, but he caught her easily and held her back, his hands around her wrists. Drew must have been playing weak the night before, letting her win. He was strong when he wanted to be.

Drew said, "I went to the group for investment advice, and I think I got it. I need to invest my time and energy in something other than my practice. After I met you, I realized I did have a problem. I was lonely."

"Being lonely sucks," she said.

"Whose clothes are these?"

"They're your clothes now. You can throw them out when you get home. They're from some guy who was passing through."

"Some guy passing through?"

She stared at him with bugged-out eyes. They were the crazy eyes she'd used to intimidate other wrestlers back in high school. "Yeah, Drew. Just some random guy. Some random guy with nice clothes."

"You can talk to me," he said.

"I have plenty of people to talk to. I have a whole group full of them." She snapped her fingers. "Get dressed. You're going to work."

He pulled off the sweatpants and tried on the clothes from the closet.

"Perfect," she said. "Do whatever you want with them. As you can see, my mom's got plenty to spare. She only keeps this stuff here in case of emergencies. Some of the big shirts make good painting smocks."

Drew tucked in the shirt then kissed Megan on the forehead. "We'll talk about this some other time."

Not likely, she thought. "Go to work and make some money so you can buy me pretty things."

He gave her a surprised look. "What would you like?"

An engagement ring, she thought. *Quickly. Before my sister gets one.*

"A boat," she said. "One of those boats that turns into a car."

"You do know I'm a doctor, right? I can get you stuff like that, if you want."

"You're a dentist," she said.

"I do all right," he insisted.

"Just go," she said, chasing him out the door. "We can talk about your dowry some other time."

Chapter 22

Sunday

On Sunday morning, Rory Taylor showed up at the house with the laundry she hadn't washed the week before.

Megan had heard, through Tina, that the previous week's debacle had blown over, but Megan was still surprised to see Rory standing on the doorstep.

Megan said, "You must be a glutton for punishment."

"I don't have laundry in my building," Rory replied, shifting the heavy-looking bag off her shoulder and dropping it.

"Does this mean we're friends again? You don't hate me?"

"Asking someone to tell you they don't hate you isn't the way to apologize," Rory said.

"I don't need to apologize. My sister already did it for me." Megan grabbed the heavy bag of clothes and nodded to Rory to come inside. "Teenie is pretty handy that way. We make a great team."

"You are the worst," Rory said.

Somewhat sarcastically, Megan said, "I love you too."

Rory shook her head. She'd grown up with Megan and Tina and knew that any attempts to talk to Megan about her behavior toward others would result in sarcasm.

They got to the laundry room, where Drew's grass-stained clothes were still sitting on the dryer from the day before.

"Those aren't your clothes," Rory said.

"They belong to Drew. He stayed over last night." She mentally edited what she'd been about to say, leaving out the details that would make Rory uncomfortable. Megan wasn't the most considerate person, but she did love Rory and didn't want to scare her off the second Sunday in a row.

"Oh," Rory said. "Okay. I guess you two are back on again."

"If he forgives me for ruining his clothes. Did you know you're supposed to put soapy stuff on grass stains before you put the clothes in the laundry?"

"Yes. Everyone knows that."

"Nobody told me."

"I'm sure lots of people told you. You probably weren't listening, as usual."

"Huh?" Megan grinned.

"Never mind."

They started sorting the clothes.

Some of Rory's things were stiff from the week before. She'd had to hang the sopping-wet clothes in her stand-up shower to dry but hadn't worn them because they weren't clean.

Megan noticed there was something different about Rory that Sunday. Not only was Rory's dark hair falling loosely around her shoulders, but she was wearing makeup, which was unusual for her.

"Rory, is that lipstick on your mouth area?"

Rory touched her face and smiled. "It's tinted gloss."

"You're wearing mascara."

"I am."

"Are you going to tell me what's going on, or do I have to drag it out of you one syllable at a time?"

"I can't explain it," she said. "I wanted to look nice."

"For laundry day with me? I'm so flattered, but I gotta be honest." She patted Drew's clothes. "I've already got someone I'm wrestling with on the front lawn."

"I might go by the antiques store later," Rory said. "They're getting some new stuff from an auction, and I'm looking at a dresser."

"What antiques store? Since when do you put on makeup to go shopping?"

"Sweet Caroline's," she said. "I've been talking to the guy who works there."

Megan put together the clues and sucked in air excitedly. "You've got a thing for Short Duncan?"

"Shush." Rory looked around nervously.

"Rory, we're in my laundry room. We're not in the high school cafeteria. Duncan's not going to hear us talking about him."

"It's nothing." She shook her head, her dark curls twirling. "I'm buying some furniture. That's all."

"You dirty girl. Talking about your personal, intimate furniture desires with a full-grown man. I'm assuming Duncan's full-grown, and that's as tall as he's going to get."

Rather than get irritated at Megan, Rory smiled. It was a sly, knowing smile. "Duncan told me you'd say something about his height."

"Whaaaaat?" Megan stopped sorting clothes. "You two talked about me?"

"We talked about you a lot," Rory said. "That's pretty much all we talk about."

"Did he make any of those weird jokes about his hot stepmom?"

Rory's smile grew. "Yes, he did. He's funny. I like his sense of humor."

"It didn't make you uncomfortable?"

She shrugged. "He makes me laugh. He does a great impression of you." She stopped talking and covered her mouth. "Oh no. I shouldn't have told you that."

"I'm flattered," Megan said.

She wasn't.

They went back to sorting laundry.

After a few minutes, Megan asked, "What else did you and Short Duncan talk about? Tell me everything."

"He likes electronic music."

"And?"

"Well, mostly we just talked about you."

"I'm so glad my humiliation is such a great icebreaker for you two."

Rory got a big grin that lit up the whole laundry room. "You gave us so much material."

"I'm so glad," Megan repeated. She was still not glad.

They set the washing machine running and went to the kitchen for food.

Rory hadn't brought the usual donuts, so the girls made croissants. Tina had never been interested in baking, but Megan and the undocumented third sister, Rory, had learned all the secrets of pastry-making from Lois Gardenia. Lois had worked as a baker before buying the flower shop.

As they were folding the second load while the fourth load washed and the third load dried, Rory asked Megan, "How can you tell if a guy's using you?"

Megan hadn't noticed that Rory got more chatty when all the machines were running. There was something about the noise of the washer and dryer going at the same time while her hands were in motion, folding, that made some of her rigid boundaries fade away.

"That's easy," Megan answered. "Is he a guy? If he is, and you're a girl, then he's using you."

Rory sighed. "I don't know why I even ask you things."

"We're all using people," Megan said. "That's how the world goes around. You're using me right now for friendship because your top choice, Tina, is always hanging out with Luca."

"I'm not using you," Rory said.

"Would you be here if you had laundry at your rat-infested apartment building?"

Rory didn't answer.

"Exactly," Megan said. "Drew was here last night because he's using me."

"You shouldn't let him do that."

"I'm getting plenty out of the arrangement, so I don't mind."

"Do you think he's using you for S-E-X?"

Megan nodded at the grass-stained clothes. "He ain't comin' here for the laundry services." She added, "Unlike some people."

"That's sad." Rory looked down. "It's not right for someone to use someone else for their body."

"He's not just using me for my body," Megan said. "He's also using me as Prozac. Yesterday morning, Drew basically told me his life was all bleak like a black-and-white movie, and then I came into the picture and started rocking his world in Technicolor."

"That's not using someone," Rory said. "That's happiness."

"No. It's like a drug. I'm like a drug. But the effect on a guy only lasts for a while. When the drug high wears off, where does that leave me?"

"I don't think that's…" Rory trailed off, confused.

"You've never had a boyfriend, and you've never done drugs, so this is all a foreign concept to you. How can I put this in a metaphor you can understand?" Megan thought about it then went with the first idea that popped into her head, as she usually did. "I'm like cheap birthday cake. I'm the corner slice with all the icing. Drew is the greedy kid at the party. He wants me, the chunky corner piece with all the icing, but he's going to get a stomach ache, and soon, he's going to want his plain sandwiches again."

Rory looked down, and there was only the sound of the washer and dryer.

Finally, she looked up, her eyes sad and hopeful at the same time, and said, "You're not cake."

"But I'm not exactly Tina, am I? I'm not the marrying kind. I'll never get a guy as good as Luca. Nobody's going to sell out the flower shop just to take me on a date. I'm the girl they call to help them fix a flat tire."

"That's not true. Duncan said some nice things about you."

"Shut up!" Megan howled with laughter. "He did not. Either you're lying, or he is."

"I'm serious. He said you're very interesting."

"He doesn't mean it. He'd say anything to get into your panties."

Rory winced at the mention of underwear. Then came a second reaction. Her eyes glistened with tears at the implication that Duncan was only after one thing.

Megan, who was looking right at Rory's face from only a few feet away, recognized the emotions on Rory's face from the times she'd been hurt herself. A bad feeling rose up in Megan. A shame sensation. She didn't know what it was, but she definitely wanted it to go away.

Without thinking about the words, Megan said to Rory, "I'm sorry I said that."

Rory's head jerked back, and her eyes widened. Rory noticed something strange was happening.

Megan also felt a shift.

Neither girl could put their finger on it, but something had changed. Something big.

Never before had Megan uttered those five words: *I'm sorry I said that.*

The two didn't talk again until it was time to eat something besides croissants, and they didn't talk about the apology. That would have felt uncomfortable for both of them. Instead, they argued about which place had the best pizza delivery.

Chapter 23

Monday

The bridezilla in Gardenia Flowers was winding up for a big fight with the big guns.

But then Megan Gardenia disarmed her with five simple words. "I'm sorry I said that."

Bridezilla fired a blank and dropped her arms. "What?"

"I shouldn't have said that," Megan said. "It was wrong of me." She was really getting the hang of the whole apology thing.

Bridezilla cocked her head to the side, listening.

Megan said, "Combining red and pink in the bridesmaid bouquets isn't the choice I would make for myself, personally, but my sister loves that combination, and she has impeccable taste." Megan gathered some pink and red roses and started remaking the sample arrangement. "If I can't get the look right for you, I'll have my sister help," she said. "My sister and I make a great team. Just like I'm sure you and your husband-to-be will make."

Bridezilla's angry face disappeared, transforming her back into a regular, middle-aged woman named Brenda. Brenda was getting married for the third time and wanted to get things right.

"Oh," Brenda said, softening like butter in the sun. "Or we could try mixing the pink with white, like you suggested. I'm open to ideas."

Megan grinned. "I bet you are. That's why you're on husband number three, huh?"

Brenda's face froze. For a moment, Megan thought she might have to roll out her new magical catchphrase yet again, but then the tension broke, and

Brenda laughed. "I may be too open-minded at times," she said. "It has gotten me into trouble."

"Don't be ashamed of your bad-girl self," Megan said. "Nice girls don't make history."

"I have a fridge magnet with that on it," Brenda said. She watched Megan work for a few minutes then said, "I do like the pink and white together."

"Let's try the pink and red as well. Let's try all the combinations. This is your third wedding, and we're going to get it right this time!"

Brenda laughingly went along with it.

An hour later, when Tina popped out of the office to check on Megan and the customer, she seemed surprised at how smoothly things were going.

Another hour later, after Brenda had left the store in good spirits, Tina came out of the office again.

Tina squinted at her sister and asked, "Are you drinking? You know the rules. If you have wine here, you have to share."

"I'm not drinking," Megan said. "I'm in a good mood. I'm as surprised as anyone at how well that went."

"Maybe not as much as me. You really turned it around. I heard how things started out with Bridezilla Brenda. I only stuck around because I thought I might have to haul one of you off the other one."

"You're the one who wrestles customers," Megan said.

"Technically, Luca was the customer, and Jessica Fitzgibbon was the gift recipient."

"I wish I'd been here that day and seen it," Megan said dreamily.

"What is with you today?"

"Rory didn't tell you? My dentist made another house call on Friday night. And a couple of times on Saturday morning."

Tina shook her head. "You two are on-again, off-again, on-again. I can't keep track of you and your guys."

"It's just one guy," Megan said. "I'm not even juggling. I've changed, Teenie. I'm a changed woman."

Tina crossed her arms and raised an eyebrow. "You've changed?"

"I've turned over a new leaf. I'm nice now. I apologize. I'll have to get a new nickname."

Tina tapped her fingers on her elbow. "Howard called this morning about some tax installments," she said.

"And?" Megan hoped Howard hadn't blabbed about their brief consult, but she knew by the look on her sister's face that he had.

"He told me about his visit from *Hilda Horsetrousers*. Really, Meenie? Using a fake name?"

"The ends justify the means."

"With you, they always do," Tina said. "This change of yours, did it happen before or after you terrorized our accountant?"

"After," Megan said. "Definitely after."

"Leave Howard alone. He's the only one who's anal enough to be trustworthy."

"That's what I said! Why is it okay when you say it but not when I do?"

"Because I didn't date the poor man and then set his car on fire."

Megan pointed her finger emphatically. "*That* was an accident."

"With you, it always is," Tina said.

Megan grabbed Tina's purse and started going through it.

Tina asked, "What do you think you're doing?"

"I'm hungry, and you always have candy."

"Check the zippered pocket."

Chapter 24

Tuesday

When Megan Gardenia strolled into work Tuesday afternoon, Tina said, "There you are! I've been calling you."

"Mr. Phone took a swim when I was dropping the kids off at the pool."

"What?"

Megan held up a bag of rice containing her damp phone. "Mr. Phone went for a dive and a backstroke in Mr. Toilet. Don't worry, I'd already flushed when it happened."

"Not again," Tina said, exasperated. "Why does that always happen to you?"

"I blame Mr. Toilet. He has a gravitational pull that cannot be explained by modern science. We should get a team of researchers into the house to conduct tests." Megan plopped the bag of rice and phone on the counter. "What were you calling me about?"

Tina did an excited dance. "Your dentist came by looking for you."

"You met him? You met my Drew?"

"Oh, Meenie, he's so cute. Why didn't you tell me he was so cute?"

"I'm not shallow like you."

Tina said, "He's a good one, Meenie. I think he might be *the one*."

"Don't be gross. You know I hate stuff like that. If you and Luca start saying you're *soul mates*, I'm going to throw up every time."

"Aren't you going to ask what we talked about?"

"He'd better not be buying me flowers from my own store. It's cute when Luca does it, but he's Luca.

That sort of behavior from a man as dignified as Dr. Drew Morgan will not stand with me."

"Don't worry. I told him not to ever buy you flowers or chocolates or any of that romantic stuff."

Megan frowned. "None of it?"

"And I didn't say anything embarrassing to him about our past." Tina chewed her lower lip in that telltale way she did when she knew she'd done something Megan wouldn't like.

Megan figured it out instantly, and yelled, "Teenie!"

"He asked," Tina said. "What was I supposed to do? You know I don't lie. That's why I made you deal with Bridezilla Brenda yesterday. She has the worst taste."

"What did he want to know?"

"I told him who the clothes in Mom's closet belonged to."

Megan considered all the things Tina might have told Drew about and concluded that telling him about the clothes wasn't the worst thing after all.

"What did he say after that?"

Tina took a bag of gummy candies from her purse and opened it on the counter between them.

"He said it must have been hard growing up without a dad around," Tina said. "He also said it explained a few things."

"He what! How long was he in here, Teenie? Was there anything you two didn't talk about? This is an invasion of my privacy." Megan grabbed the bag and fished out all the fuzzy peaches.

"If you didn't want him to ask me about Dad, you should have told him yourself," Tina said. "Being open and honest is really important in a relationship. You have to be vulnerable with each other."

"No you don't," Megan said. "Being weak is not attractive."

"Being vulnerable isn't the same as being weak."

"Yeah, it is." Megan went to the flower shop's computer, tapped at the keys furiously, and pulled up the definitions for *vulnerable* and *weak*. "Look," she said, turning the screen toward her sister's face. "They're synonyms."

Tina held up both hands. "I stand corrected. Forgive me for trying to give you dating advice. You and Drew have had plenty of successful dates now."

"That's right. Lots of them."

Tina tapped her chin thoughtfully. "Or have you? Let's see. You saw each other a couple times at your loser group therapy—always a good sign, if you ask me—and then you had that date at the pub, where you threw a drink in his face. Then you used pliers to pull off your cap so you could feed him vodka and seduce him at the house—the dental angle was a new twist, but I'm familiar with that move of yours. And then, hmm, you know, I don't believe you had another date before the next time you slept with him. Not unless you lied to me about taking yourself for a solo date to the movie on Friday."

Megan shook a fuzzy peach at Tina. "You think you're so smart. And you think you know me, but you don't."

"Meenie, if I don't know you, who does?"

Megan did not care for her sister's attitude, her tone, or any of the grains of truth she'd been blowing way, way, way out of proportion. But she was curious.

"Teenie, if you know me so well, tell me what I'm supposed to do to make Drew fall madly in love with me."

"That's easy," Tina said.

"If it's so easy, tell me. Explain it to me like I'm an idiot."

"Well," Tina said slowly. "It's very simple. Whenever you find yourself doing or saying something that Aunt Jane would do, stop. Don't do it."

Megan didn't get it. She said, "Aunt Jane is a nasty old cow who hates men."

"Exactly," Tina said.

"But I love men," Megan said.

Tina crossed her arms. "Do you? Really?"

"Get out of here," Megan said. "And take your gross candy. I'm dating a dentist. I can't be eating candy all the time. It's bad optics."

Tina picked up the bag.

Megan snatched it back. "At least leave me a couple pieces," she said. "Don't be stingy."

Tina walked away, hands raised. "Keep the bag," she said. "And call Drew. I promised him you'd call."

"I don't have his number." Megan waved at her bag of rice and phone.

"Call him at his office from the store line." Tina pointed at Megan as she headed toward the door. "Don't mess this one up. Don't be like Aunt Jane."

Chapter 25

Wednesday

The next day, Dr. Drew Morgan walked into Gardenia Flowers and up to the counter. "I hear someone's been eating a lot of candy," he said.

Megan gave him a guilty look. "Who told you?"

"A little birdie told me." He picked up the empty bag that had been on the counter since the day before and sniffed it. "Also, if you're going to eat this junk, you need to hide the evidence better."

"That's my sister's. She ate most of it. I swear. Some of it, anyway."

He set down the bag and leaned across the counter for a kiss. "I'm glad you called me yesterday," he said. "I was worried when I didn't hear from you. I thought maybe you were paying me back for that stupid text message I sent you when I was fishing with Jim."

"I didn't want to call you at work, but I didn't have your other number because my phone bit the green weenie."

"You can always call me at work," he said. "It was nice to hear your voice. It's always nice to hear something besides people screaming in pain."

"What?"

"Just some dentist humor," he said.

"There's such a thing as dentist humor?"

"Ask me sometime for my routine about wisdom teeth versus stupid teeth."

Megan laughed.

"Gotcha," he said. "If you like that, you'll love the whole routine. It's better if my hands are in your mouth so you can't beg me to stop."

She waggled her eyebrows. "I'd never tell you to stop." She nodded at the walk-in cooler. "Want to take this conversation in there and see if we can fog up all the glass?"

"Yes," he said. "But regrettably, I do have to get back to work, and I can't show up with grass stains all over my clothes."

"We don't have any grass in that cooler, but I can't make any promises about pollen staining your nice suit or rose petals getting into your crevices."

"Rose petals in my crevices? That sounds uncomfortable," he said.

"If you're going to have that kind of an attitude about it, it probably will be."

He chuckled, looked down, and fidgeted with the empty candy bag, rolling it up.

"Hey, don't eat any candy on Saturday," he said. "I'm throwing a dinner party at my house, and you're coming over."

"I am, huh? I kinda like it when you tell me what to do. For such a pretty boy, you sure can play butch."

He took a pen from the pen cup and wrote an address on a Post-it Note. "This is the house I live in with my brother. I just want to prepare you ahead of time, before you see the place. I do okay as a dentist, but my brother's the one who put up the down payment. He's a software engineer. He sold a few apps."

Megan checked the address and nodded. "He sold more than a few apps," she said.

"When you meet him, you should pretend that sort of thing impresses you, and that you think he's cooler than me. I'll know you're faking it, of course, but he could use the self-esteem boost. The dinner party is in honor of his birthday. He's turning the big three-oh, and he's not very happy about getting older."

"Can I sit on his lap and sing him Happy Birthday?"

Drew tugged on his collar. "Uh, if you think it's appropriate. I mean, if you feel, in the moment, that the moment is right."

"Stop sweating. I'm not going to sit on your brother's lap," she said. "That's something my aunt would do. Aunt Jane is hilarious. You'd love her."

"She sounds fun. Do you want to bring her? We've got a big table, and I can set an extra chair."

"No way," Megan said. "I wouldn't inflict that on you or your brother."

"Seven o'clock," he said. "Don't bring any food or wine."

"Are you trying to use reverse psychology on me?"

"Not at all," he said. "My brother always gets enough food and wine to feed an army. All you need to bring is your gorgeous self."

"And I will. Wearing nothing but a trench coat," she said.

"Please wear clothes."

"Can I wear my I Love Beijing T-shirt?"

He shrugged. "Sure. Why not?" He leaned over the counter and kissed her again. "Thanks," he said.

"Thanks for what?"

"For being you."

"You're welcome," she said. "And I do know what you mean. I'm the corner piece of cake with all the icing."

"You sure are." He winked at her then turned and walked to the door. On his way out, he yelled back, "No more candy!"

Chapter 26

Dr. Drew Morgan

When Dr. Morgan got back to the dental office, he stopped by Candy's desk. Candy was his office manager, and the two were very close, so he felt comfortable digging around in her desk drawers while she wasn't there.

The irony of having an office manager named Candy working for the dental practice was made only more entertaining by the fact that Candy always kept bags of candy in her desk. She didn't nibble it that much, but she liked having it there "just in case." There were times their diabetic patients had drops in blood sugar, such as after a stressful procedure in the chair, and it kept them from fainting on the way out, or—worse—before they could pay their bill.

Candy returned from her lunch break just in time to catch Drew with his hand in the candy drawer, which was technically Candy's candy drawer.

"Naughty!" She slapped his wrist. "I'll tell your dad." Dr. Morgan worked at the same practice as Dr. Morgan Senior, though the senior Morgan only worked part-time those days.

"Just three pieces, then I'll brush my teeth right after," Dr. Morgan said.

"And floss," she said.

"Who's the dentist here?"

She replied, "Who's the person who knows the truth about you? The one who knows that you only floss about half as often as you recommend to all your patients?"

Drew ignored her ribbing and sat on her desk while he popped a candy into his mouth.

Candy said, "What's gotten into you? You're humming all the time."

"I'm in a good mood."

"But why? You had Mr. Donnelly this morning and Mrs. Albert. You should be raiding my other drawer, where I keep the hard liquor."

"I'm seeing a girl," he said. "You'll meet her at Alan's birthday dinner on Saturday."

"Does Charlotte know?"

"It's none of Charlotte's business. It's barely yours. I'm only telling you because you have candy, and because you'll be meeting her anyway."

Candy narrowed her eyes at her boss. "Does this have anything to do with the unpaid house call you shoved through the system on the weekend when you thought I wouldn't notice?"

"I was going to tell you about that," he said.

"You should never date a patient," she said. "Or at least if you do, you should warn me, so I can purge her records and keep your dad from finding out."

"She's not a patient," Drew said. "We met outside of work, and she needed an excuse to see me, so she used a pair of pliers and pulled off one of her caps."

Candy gasped and covered her mouth. "No way."

"I shouldn't be telling you this," he said. "Why do I keep doing this? Whenever she's not around, I'm always talking about her. Last Friday, I was with the old rugby team, and I wouldn't shut up about her. You know how those guys are. They kept asking questions. I may have said too much."

"Your rugby buddies? Those guys are disgusting."

"I know," he said. "We had a good time catching up, and we had some laughs, but I'm not going to hang out with them anymore."

"Not when you've got a new woman in your life," Candy said.

He ate another sweet. If he was going to have to brush and floss his teeth, he wanted it to be worth it.

"Tell me more about her," Candy said. "What's her name?"

He started to say Meenie but then said Megan. That was her name, after all. The other name was a nickname and not a flattering one.

"She runs a flower store with her sister," he said. "I stopped by there today. It's a cute place. I…" He trailed off. Picturing the flower store in his mind had brought up a memory of writing down his house address. Had he transposed the last two digits again? He made that mistake half the time.

The phone rang, interrupting both the conversation and Drew's worries he'd given Megan the wrong address.

Candy answered the phone then yanked the bag of candy from Drew's hand and threw it back into her drawer.

Drew went off to brush his teeth and daydream about Megan. He even flossed.

Chapter 27

Friday

On Friday night, Rory and Megan met up at O'Flannigan's for drinks after work.

Rory said, "I think Luca's going to propose to Tina. He was asking me if she likes big, romantic gestures, or if she prefers things more casual."

Megan, who knew for a fact that Luca *was* going to propose since she'd been helping him shop for a ring, feigned ignorance.

"It's too soon," Megan said. "They haven't even dated for a year. I wouldn't worry about it."

"I'm not worried," Rory said. "Do you think she'd ask us to be her bridesmaids?"

"If she knows what's good for her."

The waitress came by, and Rory said, "I'll have the linguini."

Megan gave Rory a stunned, wide-eyed look then said to the waitress, "I'll also have the linguini. It's a special occasion. To heck with all the carbs. Who's counting?"

The waitress said, "We do have a low-carb linguine made with zucchini noodles."

Megan gasped in horror. "Leave us now, and I'll pretend you didn't say that."

The waitress laughed. People had been laughing at Megan's jokes a lot more lately.

After the waitress left with their order, Megan said to Rory, "People have been laughing at my jokes lately. I must be getting funnier."

Rory said, "People tend to laugh if the jokes are actually funny and not just mean."

"I don't get it," Megan said. "Jokes are supposed to be mean. If you take that away, all that's left is puns."

"You have been funnier lately," Rory said. "More light and playful. Less aggressive."

"You take that back," Megan said.

"I like this new, softer side of you."

"Gross. Don't make me say your no-no words." Megan reached into her tote bag and tossed a slim paperback to Rory. "There's that stupid book you were asking about."

"The one you keep in the bathroom? Thanks!" Rory opened the dog-eared old copy of *The Secret Rules of Love* and started scanning the pages.

Megan said, "You're not really going to use those tricks on Duncan, are you?"

Rory's eyes flicked up. "You called him Duncan. Not Short Duncan."

"He knows he's short." Megan took a sip of her Bloody Mary. "Seriously, are you actually reading that book for real? It's a joke. No self-respecting modern woman would believe any of that old-fashioned junk. We only keep it around the house for laughs."

"There's lots of good advice in here. I read it whenever I'm in your bathroom." She flipped to the summary and read a few of the rules out loud. "Meenie, I think you broke an awful lot of these rules with Drew."

"So what?" Megan played with the salt and pepper shaker. "Which ones? Tell me which rules I broke."

"You got intimate right away, and you tell him what to do, and you've seen him twice in a week." Rory glanced up, panicked. "Is he married? It says not to date a married man."

"What kind of a girl do you think I am?"

"You tell me. You broke so many of the other rules."

"He's not married. He had a two-year dry spell before he met me. Before that, he was only with one person, a girl he knew since high school. They grew apart. He says she was cold, whatever that means."

"Wow." Rory looked impressed. "You guys actually talked, in between the other stuff."

"Enough about me. Why are you having linguini?"

"Because I like it."

"But why were you able to ask for it by name instead of pointing at the menu and grunting like a caveman?"

Rory reached into her purse and pulled out a small bottle of pills. "I'm taking anti-anxiety medication."

"Does that stuff work? A lot of people at the group take it, and they're still messed up."

"People respond differently," Rory said. "My alternative health doctor says I'm an undermethylator. I have a hard time breaking down folates."

Megan snorted. "Sounds like a big pile of made-up pseudoscience to sell a bunch of supplements. Did she take into account your astrological sign too?"

Rory's face fell. She put the pills away and muttered something about people being different.

Megan quickly recognized the feeling of shame she felt over Rory's reaction. "I'm sorry I said that," Megan said. The phrase was coming out more and more easily. "That was my stupid, knee-jerk response. Honestly, I didn't mean it."

Rory looked away. "If you didn't mean it, then why'd you say it?"

"Because I'm an idiot," Megan said. "And because I'm scared of people taking advantage of you, Rory."

"Okay." Rory rubbed her eyebrow and avoided eye contact.

"Tell me more about your alternate health doctor," Megan said. "I promise to shut my big mouth and keep an open mind."

"Are you sure? We could talk about something else."

"It's important," Megan said. "I'm really glad you're feeling better, and it makes me happy to see you talking about a guy, even if it is Duncan. So, tell me about your vitamins."

"It's prescription medicine. From a doctor," Rory said, and she went on to give Megan a surprisingly understandable primer on epigenetics.

Megan found herself in the surprisingly rare position of witnessing another human being taking control of her life, and it struck her with awe. It was like watching some beautiful piece of art being created.

After the linguini and a couple of Bloody Marys, Megan announced that she needed to use the ladies' room. The phrase "drain the lizard" was used, much to Rory's horror. Rory had already been, so she stayed at the table while Megan went on her own. Neither of them were the type of girl who needed a companion for the bathroom anyway.

On her way back to their table, Megan spotted a familiar-looking group of guys. They were laughing over a pitcher of beer at a large table. These were the same guys Drew had played rugby with when he was younger, the guys he'd been hanging out with the previous Friday.

Megan had to pass by them, and when she did, one of them caught her by the arm.

"I know you," he said. The guy had red hair, and he was missing a front tooth. No stump. Just a blank spot.

Megan replied, "If you don't let go of my arm, you'll be getting to know my foot in your face."

He released her, drunkenly slurred something about her being a real tiger, and the whole group laughed.

"You don't know me," she said.

Red gave her a leering look. "You're that girl Andrew told us about." He said to the others, "This is her. The little wildcat."

Another of the guys said, "I'd put up with a little scratching for a taste of that. Our boy Andrew has some good taste."

Red undressed her with his eyes. "Next time you pull out one of your teeth, give me a call. I'll take your mind off it."

Megan should have walked away and left the unpleasant interaction at that, but Megan Gardenia wasn't one to walk away from a fight.

She demanded to know what Drew—the guy they called Andrew—had told them about her.

The guys were only too happy to repeat back about ninety percent of her interactions with Drew with a fifty percent accuracy rate. She didn't know if the inaccuracy was hyperbole on Drew's part or just their beer-addled imaginations, but none of it painted her in a very flattering light.

"C'mon over here and join us," Red said, patting his lap. "Andrew said you're the kind of girl who likes to party. That's the kind of girl we like."

Megan stepped in close enough to smell his beer breath. "You want me on your lap, Red? You think you could handle all of this, even after everything Andrew Morgan told you?"

Red's face became even stupider looking as he assured her he could handle whatever she was dishing out.

"Close your eyes," she said.

He did.

She dumped the contents of the group's beer pitcher on his lap.

The group of guys erupted in noise, laughter, and jeers.

Megan stomped her way back to the table where Rory was sitting.

As Megan crossed in front of the bar, she heard Gary Jackson, the owner of the pub, yelling, "Megan Gardenia! Not again! You're banned until Christmas!"

Chapter 28

Megan decided not to say anything to Drew about his friends and their behavior. Things were going well in her life, and she'd turned over a new leaf. She was light and playful, not aggressive.

Old Megan would have torn a strip off Drew and insisted he defend her honor by annihilating all of his rugby buddies. She would have done so in the least efficient way possible—over approximately one thousand text messages, sent rapid-fire in between vodka shots.

New Megan didn't send Drew a bunch of crazy text messages. She didn't even touch the vodka. When she got home Friday night, she ranted at Muffins then tossed and turned all night in bed, dreaming about dumping larger and larger quantities of stuff on the heads of Red and his rugby buddies.

She woke up Saturday morning feeling worse than she should have, considering she'd only had a couple of drinks with dinner. All that indignant outrage had shot up her stress hormones, which had given her a heady buzz the night before, but now she was coming down.

She checked her phone, which had recovered from its last soaking, to make sure she hadn't sent any of the angry text messages she'd been composing in her fitful dreams.

She hadn't.

That was great news!

She did have a horrible rage hangover, but on the plus side, she hadn't tried to destroy her relationship with Drew.

Not yet, anyway.

That would happen soon enough.

Chapter 29

Saturday Morning

Dr. Drew Morgan

While Megan was getting out of bed and feeding Muffins, a couple of neighborhoods away, Drew was helping his brother, Alan, get ready for the dinner party that evening. They were polishing wineglasses. Alan didn't like the way the dishwasher left tiny spots on them.

Alan was three years younger than Drew and had made his first million dollars before Drew had finished paying off his student loans for dentist school. It was a fact Alan brought up as frequently as possible.

Alan was turning thirty that day, and he was bummed. He hadn't accomplished nearly as much as he had hoped for by that age. He'd only sold three start-up tech companies for big bucks to the industry giants.

"I've peaked," Alan said gloomily. "It's all downhill from here." He set down the wineglass he'd been polishing with a lint-free cloth.

"You're right," said Drew, who'd gotten tired of trying to give his brother pep talks. He was taking a page from Megan's playbook and trying some tough love sarcasm. "Your life is basically over. The fun part, anyway. You might as well buy some loose pants that come up to your chest, like Grandpa, and invest in a reclining chair that massages your back and other parts I wish I didn't know about."

"Grandpa does love his massaging chair," Alan said. "And he does talk about his prostate way too much."

"There you go. You've got a blueprint for the rest of your days."

"No way. I want what you've got."

"You want to do root canals while listening to light piano jazz?"

"Not that part. I want a girl like yours. I've never seen you this happy."

"Megan's a tricky one. I wouldn't say I've *got* her. I do know I'm on my toes whenever she's around. I know I'm not bored."

"She's nothing like Charlotte, is she? I didn't want to jump on the bandwagon when you guys were breaking up, but I always found Charlotte a little dull. And cold."

"Mom liked her."

Alan said nothing.

They both laughed.

Drew said, "Mom won't like Megan."

"That's a bonus," Alan said. "I love it when Mom has to pretend she likes someone she doesn't. Remember when I was dating that dancer, and I told Mom she was a stripper? Priceless. You can't buy entertainment like that." Alan went to the fridge and started pulling out things for dinner. "Charlotte was exactly like Mom," he said. "I can see why you're going in the opposite direction this time."

"I love Mom," Drew said. "I just don't want to marry her. That's why every Christmas or Valentine's Day or anniversary I had to see the disappointment on Charlotte's face when she didn't get a ring. It wasn't fair to her."

"I bumped into Charlotte the other day," Alan said. "Her finger isn't ringless anymore."

"Good for her," Drew said, and he meant it. "Anyone we know?"

"Do you know an accountant named Howard Hamilton? Charlotte gave me his card. She said when she found him, he was in ruins. Some woman did a real number on him. They were only dating a few weeks when he proposed."

"Good for her," Drew said again, but he didn't mean it as much that time. He'd been with Charlotte for a long time, and while he hadn't wanted to put a ring on her finger, hearing that some other guy *did* made him wonder if he hadn't made a huge mistake.

Alan thrust a chunk of white and blue cheese under Drew's nose. "Has this gone off? I can never tell with the moldy cheeses."

Drew, who had an excellent sense of smell, told him it was still good.

They continued to prepare for the dinner party.

Drew mentioned that Megan had a friend who worked as a caterer, and perhaps they could hire her for their next gala event. "We should have hired her for tonight," Drew said.

"But it's just a casual get-together," Alan said.

"A casual get-together with seven courses," Drew said. "You're as bad as Mom."

Alan pointed the cheese knife at his older brother. "Don't you dare. I will stab you."

Drew laughed as he went back to polishing things. They'd moved on from the stemware to the silverware.

He wondered what Megan was up to.

He told Alan about Megan's crazy cat, and Alan only wrinkled his nose. The boys hadn't had any pets growing up, due to their mother's hatred of pet hair and dirt from outside.

"He's a great cat," Drew said. "You'd like him. I wonder if Megan would bring him over tonight. Do people do that? They don't, do they? Dogs, yes, but not cats."

"You're lovesick over this girl, and it's melting your brain," Alan said.

"I wonder what she's doing now," Drew said, speaking his repetitive thoughts out loud, then, "I'm going to send her a text. Just to make sure she doesn't forget about tonight."

"You sound like Dad when you announce what you're about to do."

"Those are the perils of being a dentist," Drew said. "We get used to explaining everything we do as we're doing it. I like it when Dad does it. It's comforting."

"I never thought of it that way, but it is nice."

Drew pulled out his phone and spoke the words of his text message as he composed it.

"*Having a good Saturday? I'm helping my brother get ready for tonight's seven-course gala dinner. Don't worry, you can still wear your Beijing T-shirt. If things get too stuffy, you can liven things up by throwing a drink in someone's face.*"

"She'd better *not* throw a drink in anyone's face," Alan said. "We're serving red wine, and I have a new carpet in the dining room."

"It's just one of our little in-jokes," Drew said.

"Based on what?"

"She threw some water in my face once."

"Were you outside having a water balloon fight with a bunch of children?"

"No."

"Were you washing cars for a fundraiser?"

"No."

"Then I have to ask, big brother. Where were you, and what were you doing when this Megan girl threw a drink in your face?"

“We were talking, in a pub.”

Alan grinned. “I will pay for your entire wedding if you propose to her in front of Mom.”

Chapter 30

Megan Gardenia

To say that Dr. Drew Morgan's friendly text message to Megan was *misinterpreted* by Megan would be an understatement.

Megan's eyes read the words he'd typed: "*Having a good Saturday? I'm helping my brother get ready for tonight's seven-course gala dinner. Don't worry, you can still wear your Beijing T-shirt. If things get too stuffy, you can liven things up by throwing a drink in someone's face.*"

Megan's brain, however, read something much, much worse, thanks to the drink-throwing reference combined with her vivid recollection of the rugby guys from the night before.

In Megan's brain, the words on the screen were broken down and reformed into what she *thought* Drew meant.

Having a good Saturday? = I heard you were drunk last night as usual.

I'm helping my brother get ready for tonight's seven-course gala dinner. = I am a good person with an actual life, not a garbage person like you.

Don't worry, you can still wear your Beijing T-shirt. = Please wear your dumb shirt so my friends can laugh at you.

If things get too stuffy, you can liven things up by throwing a drink in someone's face. = I heard what you did last night to my rugby friends, and I am taking their side, because boys will be boys, and men always stick together.

To say that, in the moments following the message, Megan went a little "off the rails," sanity-wise, would have also been an understatement.

But luckily for Megan, fate intervened.

Just as she was about to press send on a hate-filled, expletive-riddled message—one which was barely legible in meaning yet in a clearly communicated tone—Mr. Toilet saved the day.

Megan's phone had only recently recovered from its last splash in the welcoming waters of Mr. Toilet, and its circuits could not withstand another dunk.

Sadly, it would be the end of things for the phone but not the relationship. Not yet. Not if Mr. Toilet had any say in the matter.

On that fateful Saturday, Mr. Toilet exerted a gravitational pull on Mr. Phone, and Mr. Phone went for another dip, slipping from Megan's hand before she could send the message to Drew.

Chapter 31

Dr. Drew Morgan

Drew put his phone away and said to his brother, "That's odd. It gave me those dots, like she was composing a reply, for a long time, but then it went away, and she didn't send anything."

Alan said, "Just call her. People do too much by phones and apps. It's terrible for the human mind. Apps are ruining society."

"And yet those same apps have made you a rich man."

"Why do you think I'm so grumpy all the time? It's not about turning thirty. I may be having an existential crisis."

"I'm sorry to hear that," Drew said.

"I bought this house with blood money," Alan said.

"I'm not sure that's what blood money means." Drew patted his chest. "And I should know. Everything Dad and I purchase is bought with blood money. Teeth bleed. Gums bleed. It's all blood money."

"Stop trying to make me laugh. I'm turning thirty, and I've done nothing but contribute to the further destruction of society's fabric. I don't want to feel better."

"Get used to it. When Megan comes over, you're going to have to lighten up. She doesn't tolerate people feeling sorry for themselves and moping around. It's one of the many things I love about her."

Alan raised an eyebrow. "Love?"

"Sure," Drew said, lifting his chin. "I love many things about her. I may even love her."

"Good for you," Alan said. "I'm happy for you, bro." He put the marble cheese platters into the fridge to chill then sighed. "Now I know what I forgot," he said to the closed fridge door. "Flowers. What kind of animal throws a dinner party with no fresh flowers?"

Drew rubbed his temples. "I'm sending a psychic message to Megan. I'm asking her to bring over some flowers from the shop."

"You're crazy."

Drew closed his eyes. "I've got a good feeling about this. Megan and I got off to a bad start, but we've had excellent, clear communication with each other since then."

"Clear enough for psychic messages?"

"Can't hurt to try. What's the worst that could happen?"

Chapter 32

Megan Gardenia

When Tina showed up at the flower shop at two o'clock on Saturday, Megan was standing in the walk-in flower cooler again.

Tina slid open the glass door and asked, "Now what have you done?"

Megan, who was shivering, could only manage to say, "Mr. Toilet ate Mr. Phone again. I think he's dead."

"Your pupils don't look right," Tina said. She stepped into the cooler with Megan and closed the door. "This isn't normal," she said.

"Everyone would stand inside a flower cooler if they had one. People don't know what they're missing out on."

"You seem awfully upset over your phone."

"Mr. Phone was a good phone. We had some good times together."

"You'll learn to love another phone," Tina said.

"It won't be the same."

"You're not standing in here because of the phone, are you?"

Megan sniffed.

"We can't stay in here forever," Tina said.

"Speak for yourself."

Tina's breath was warming the front of Megan's face, which made Megan realize how cold she was, but she didn't budge.

Tina asked, "Are you going to be okay?"

Megan said, "I can't get any worse, really."

Without waiting for any explanation, Tina said, "You do know you are your own worst enemy, right? That you make things complicated for yourself?"

"Tell me how to be uncomplicated," Megan said softly.

"It's very easy. Think about what Aunt Jane would do, and then don't do that."

"You don't have to kick me while I'm down," Megan said.

"I'm not. Do you really think the people who love you are constantly giving you advice about your life because we want to see you hurt?"

Megan said, "Drew hurt my feelings."

"Oh," Tina said. "Then what happened. Did you hurt him back?"

Megan didn't answer right away. She had a feeling she was being tested. "No," she said.

"Well, that's a good sign."

Then, because Megan was feeling guilty, she added, "But only because I dropped my phone before I could send him a message telling him how I felt."

"I understand." Tina nodded. "Right into Mr. Toilet." She glanced out at the flower shop then back into her sister's eyes. "So what are you going to do next?"

"Aren't you going to ask what he did to me?"

"Does it matter? He hurt your feelings. Whether it was on purpose or by accident doesn't matter, because I'm guessing by the way you're feeling that it *feels* like he did it on purpose."

"When you put it like that, you make me sound stupid."

"Sometimes you can be stupid," Tina said. "But not all of the time. What matters the most is what you do next."

"Drew's having a dinner party tonight. I don't think I should go."

"Were you invited?"

Megan gave her sister a dirty look.

"Sorry," Tina said, smiling. "Not a good time for jokes." She looked down for a moment, then said, "Your instincts are right. If you're upset with Drew about something, it might be better to talk to him when the two of you are alone." She looked into her sister's eyes and added, "Alone together, in person. No more texting."

"Mr. Phone doesn't want to do anything for me anyway," Megan said. "Stupid men in my life, always letting me down."

Tina said, "You can always count on me."

"And Muffins."

"Do you want a hug?"

"No. But you can give me one anyway."

Megan let Tina hug her. There was nowhere else to go inside the cramped cooler.

"Let's go somewhere less chilly," Tina said, leading the way.

They emerged from the walk-in cooler.

Tina looked over the greenery that was strewn everywhere and said, "Did we get a huge order?"

"I'm working on something, and I can't make up my mind." Megan showed Tina a flower arrangement she'd been working on.

"What's this?" Tina asked. "It can't be for a wedding. None of our brides are this adventurous."

"It's to send to Drew's house for his dinner party."

"Oh. Interesting."

"I'm sending it with a note apologizing for me not being able to make it to dinner," Megan said.

Tina picked up the note card on the counter and started reading it. Her jaw dropped.

"You can't send this," Tina said.

Megan grimaced. "Is it that bad?"

Tina read some more, the color draining from her face.

"It's bad," Megan said.

Tina flicked her eyes up to meet Megan's. "Did you have Aunt Jane help you compose this masterpiece?"

"Shut up and tell me what I should write instead."

"I'll write the note," Tina said, and she did.

Tina wrote a nice note, and she kept it simple. She didn't let Megan anywhere near it.

Then Tina called their delivery company and had the bouquet, a gorgeous centerpiece, sent to Drew's house.

Chapter 33

Dr. Drew Morgan

Drew's brother, Alan Morgan, stared in disbelief at the centerpiece. "It's perfect," he said. "I need to stop thinking about apps that are going to change the world. Obviously the technology of the future is whatever frequency you and Megan are on."

"I'm not sure we're on the same frequency," Drew said. "This note doesn't sound like her. 'Sorry I can't make it to your dinner. Something came up. Talk soon, Megan.' That's not her at all. Do you think she's been kidnapped?"

"Yes. This is exactly what kidnappers do."

"Don't be sarcastic."

"No, really. I'm sure the ransom note will be along any minute."

Drew crossed his arms and started sulking.

"Don't sulk," Alan said. "That's my job. I'm the old man who's turning thirty. Poor me."

"Poor me," Drew said. "If she sent this note, it's not a good sign."

"Since when does a polite apology spell trouble?"

"When it comes from a girl who doesn't do polite apologies."

"Maybe she's changed. People change," Alan said.

"You don't actually believe that, do you?"

"No," Alan said. "She's probably going to dump you."

Drew didn't want to admit it, but he'd been thinking the same thing ever since she'd gone silent on the phone.

"You've still got me," Alan said.

"I'm going to be single forever," Drew said.

"We're *both* going to be single forever," Alan said. "Just the two of us, living in this big house we bought with our blood money."

"You have to stop saying that, or people will think we're running a crime syndicate."

Alan went over to the fridge and opened it. "You get the crackers, and I'll liberate one of the cheese plates," Alan said.

"Why?"

"Because it's too early to open the wine, and we need something to ease our sorrows. Me, turning thirty, and you over getting dumped by a girl before we even had a chance to terrorize Mom."

"I'm not sure it's too early to open the wine," Drew said. "What about letting it breathe?"

"Is that a real thing?" Alan put the marble cheese board on the polished granite counter between them and flung back the clear plastic wrap. "I thought that was just something Mom said to excuse her afternoon drinking."

Drew picked up the note from Gardenia Flowers again and frowned. The note didn't sound like Megan at all, and he was getting worried. Maybe she *had* been kidnapped.

Alan handed Drew a bottle. "Do us the honors," he said. "Put the note down. She said you would talk soon, and you will."

Chapter 34

Megan found herself at the community center for her Tuesday night self-help group, and a few things struck her as odd.

First of all, she didn't remember driving there.

Second, she was naked except for a pair of cutoff jean shorts that were too small.

When she walked into the room, the whole group turned and greeted her in unison. "Hello, Meenie. We're so glad you could make it."

A pair of bluebirds flew over to Megan, carrying an oversized T-shirt that read HONK IF YOU LOVE CHEESE. Megan was grateful for the shirt to cover her nakedness. She pulled on the shirt and joined the group.

As you may have guessed by the bluebirds, it wasn't really Tuesday night, and this wasn't really the self-help group.

It was still Saturday, and Megan was at home, in her bathtub, fast asleep. But she didn't know that yet.

In the dream, Feather was there, leading the group and looking stunning and perfect as always. She stood, swished off a magnificent gray cape she'd been wearing, and revealed an equally stunning baby, which she was holding easily with one arm while feeding. Also, Feather was over ten feet tall and growing. Motherhood really became her.

"Have a seat and join us," Feather said, her voice echoing from her great height.

Megan tugged down her T-shirt to cover what her tiny jean shorts didn't and took a seat.

She checked the spot where Drew had sat the two times he'd come to the group. He wasn't there. A mannequin, posed in a seated position, was there instead. The mannequin wore one of Drew's suits.

A woman said to Megan, "Your hair has certainly grown out nice and long."

Megan turned to find her mother, Lois Gardenia, sitting in a chair that was higher than all the other chairs, like a throne, or a lifeguard's station. Lois had a team of gorgeous men on stepladders surrounding her and grooming her like she was a movie star. One was buffing her nails, and the other one was rubbing night cream on her face.

Megan had no doubt this was her mother, and not an impostor, because the men were applying the night cream that Lois normally had smuggled into the country by registered mail.

"When did you get back in town?" Megan asked.

"That's not what I'm here to discuss," Lois Gardenia said.

Two hands covered Megan's eyes. Someone was behind her. "Guess who," someone growled in Megan's ear.

"Aunt Jane," Megan said, recognizing the woman's gravelly voice instantly.

Jane Gardenia shoved an extra chair into the circle and joined the group next to Megan. She was wearing a T-shirt proclaiming her love of Beijing, a city she'd never been to.

The whole group said, in unison, "Hello, Aunt Jane. Thank you for joining us."

Feather switched her baby to the other side of her chest. Someone handed her a second matching baby, which she cradled on the other side. "These are my babies," Feather said, even though nobody had asked. "I had a natural birth."

The group said, "Hello, babies. Thank you for joining us."

Megan turned toward her mother to roll her eyes about Feather, but her mother was very far away. There was a conveyer belt, like the kind that were at some airports, running through the middle of the group. Lois Gardenia, her assistants, and the tall chair were moving away, slowly but smoothly.

Ryan was sitting next to the edge of the conveyer belt, unaware that the end of his scarf was dangling only inches away.

Aunt Jane squeezed Megan's knee and said in her gravelly voice, "Your father called today. I answered the phone. He said to wish a belated birthday to Teenie and an early one to you for next month."

"Daddy called?" Megan had her little-girl voice back. "You talked to Daddy?"

"That man has no man parts," Aunt Jane said. "He doesn't deserve to be called Daddy."

Megan raised her tiny, weak, little-girl arm slowly, pointing her finger at her aunt. "You and Mom drove him away."

Aunt Jane took a deep drag off a cigarette she'd produced by magic and said, "How would you know that? You were just a tiny baby."

"Why else would he leave? You and Mom drove him away. Everything was fine until you moved in with us."

"No it wasn't," Aunt Jane said. "I moved in with your mother to help her pay the bills and raise you girls, but it was after your father left. If anyone drove him away, it was you and your sister. You were so demanding."

"We were not," Megan said. "We were normal. Normal little girls. All we wanted was to be loved."

Aunt Jane took another long drag. "Is that all you want?"

"That's all I want," Megan said.

"Then what are you doing here?" Aunt Jane asked. "Why are you in therapy?"

"I wanted to lose five pounds."

"Why are you still here?"

"I keep coming to this group so they can help me to be a better person."

Aunt Jane said, "You don't have to make yourself perfect before you deserve love. That's what I'm always telling Lois. At last, she finally listened to me, and look at her now." Aunt Jane waved to the tiny figures on the tall chair in the distance. "She has to beat them away with a stick."

Megan looked over at Feather, who was now twenty feet tall and nursing a half a dozen babies at her incredibly long torso. She had multiple arms with which to hold them.

"Is that true?" Megan asked the towering figure. "Can a person deserve love even when they haven't become the person they want to be?"

Feather said, "Love is love."

"That is not helpful," Megan said. "Why can't you ever come right out and tell someone what their problem is? Why do you only ask questions instead of giving us the answers we want? Are we not paying you enough? Is five dollars not enough to get a single sentence telling us what we're supposed to do? You're the professional! You're supposed to know best!"

"There's a stack of books by the door," Feather said. "Babies recognize the sound of their mother's voice from the moment they are born. They learned it inside the womb. They learn from their mother."

Suddenly, Megan found herself at the door, picking up the books. They were all written in a nonsense language, and yet they made perfect sense.

She leafed through the top six. Now she knew everything. At last, it was all crystal clear.

Megan yanked open the door to the community center hallway.

In real life, she moaned and twitched in the tub.

Out in the real world, Muffins sat on the ledge of the tub, watching his mistress in between dozing and waking up to sample the bathwater.

Megan twitched and moaned for ten minutes in real time. In the dream world, hours passed as she ran up and down hallways, trying to find Drew.

Then she slept peacefully for a while, her nose safely above the waterline.

Eventually, when the water had cooled below a comfortable temperature, Megan woke up with a start.

Everything from the dream and from real life collided, and she knew what she had to do.

She groaned loudly while emerging from the waters, like a swamp beast preparing to attack a mob of angry villagers.

Muffins bolted.

Chapter 35

It was raining and dark at nine o'clock on Saturday when Megan pulled her mother's dented old Cadillac onto Drew's street.

She hadn't been to his house before, but she remembered the address from when he'd written it on the notepad at the store.

She banged on the door of the house she believed to be Drew's. All the lights were on, and she could see people sitting inside at a dining room table.

A woman with silver hair answered the door. "Can I help you, dear?"

"Is this Drew Morgan's house?"

"Do you mean the doctor?"

"He's a dentist," Megan said, then, "Yes. The doctor."

"He's across the street. He must be giving people the wrong address. We received some beautiful flowers for him earlier today. I'll have to speak to him about that."

Megan pulled away, back out into the rain, but came back. "You liked the flowers?"

"They were stunning," the woman said. "I wrote down the name of the florist so I could order from them for my next party."

Megan grinned. "I'd kiss you right now, but I'm saving it up." She turned and ran back out into the rain. "Have a great dinner!"

The cold rain was coming down hard as she crossed the wide, tree-lined street to get to Drew's house.

Megan banged on the door and rang the doorbell at the same time.

The door opened.

A man who looked a lot like Drew, except with glasses, stood in the doorway.

"Let me guess," he said. "You must be—"

"No time for your games, bro," Megan said as she ducked around him and inside.

She kicked off her sneakers and rounded a corner at top speed, navigating to the dining room based on smell alone.

She took a left down a hallway and ran into a person. They both fell to the floor.

Megan helped up the person, who was a young woman about her age.

"Oh no," the young woman said, waving her hands in front of her face desperately. "I knocked out your tooth."

Megan let out a curse word. The cap had fallen off her tooth. She felt the ugly stump with the tip of her tongue, then cursed again.

"Don't worry," the young woman said. "This is my boss's house, and he's a dentist. You're lucky you were in the right spot when…" She trailed off as she gave Megan a more careful look. "You're her," she said. "Aren't you?"

"I probably am."

"You're the one who pulled her dental cap off with a pair of pliers. I know all about you. I'm Drew's office manager. I know everything. I heard all about you."

"All good things, I hope."

"He won't stop talking about you. The patients love it. They like it when Dr. Morgan tells them what's going on in his life rather than asking those polite, inane questions they can't answer with tools in their mouth."

"He's a real blabbermouth, that one." Megan thought, angrily, of the rugby guys. Drew had exposed her to them!

In the next instant, though—it was a night of self-revelation for Megan—she realized that the rugby guys might have taken a small amount of what Drew had truthfully told them and blown it out of proportion themselves. That would account for some of the inaccuracies in their stories.

It was tempting for Megan to see everything in black and white, with absolute certainty, following her basic rules. If she hurt someone else's feelings, they couldn't take a joke. If someone hurt *her* feelings, they had done so deliberately.

But she was starting to understand that sometimes she hurt people's feelings on purpose, and it wasn't always a joke. For that, she would apologize, and she would try to lash out less.

When it came to people hurting her, she had to leave their motivations open to more interpretation, more investigation, more understanding. She had to think about what Aunt Jane would do then not do that.

The young woman said, "Did you arrange the flowers for the centerpiece? It's gorgeous. I can't do anything artistic. You're so lucky to have your talents and to get to play with pretty flowers all day."

"The buckets can be heavy, but I'm pretty lucky," Megan said.

"My name's Candy," the woman said, offering her hand. "I'm Drew's office manager."

"You work at a dental office, and your name is Candy."

"That's right," Candy said. "I basically grew up with the Morgan boys. My mom was the bookkeeper for Dr. Morgan, Senior. She was working for the family before I was even born." Candy picked up something from the floor. "Your tooth," she said. "I should get back to dinner. We started late, and we're only halfway through the courses. Alan really outdid himself this time. How about you stay here, and I'll send the doctor back so he can fix your tooth before you meet everyone?"

"That's a good idea. He can fix *ma toof*."

Candy ushered Megan into the powder room then went off to get Drew.

When Drew walked in, he immediately hugged her. "You're wet, and you're freezing cold." He hugged her tighter, not caring that the rain was soaking into his clothes.

"It's raining out," she said.

"The flowers you sent made my brother happy." He released the hug then grabbed her hands and warmed them both between his palms. "I'm so glad you're here. I'd much rather have you than flowers. What happened? I was worried you'd been kidnapped."

"Drew, I need to tell you something."

"Please don't dump me," he said. "I know it's not very manly to beg but please don't. Whatever you have to say, we can work it out."

"I'm not dumping you."

"But? There's always a *but*."

"But I might have a problem or two. I think it comes from family stuff. Surprise surprise, right?"

"Everyone's got some baggage," he said.

"My father left us when I was too small to even remember him. To me, he was just this guy who sent us money for stuff. He wasn't a deadbeat. He paid alimony and child support, even though he and my mom were never officially married. He just moved across the country and settled in with his new family, so he didn't have time for us."

"That's awful."

"My aunt and my mother used to fight about which one of them drove him away, but, Drew?"

"Yes?" His brown eyes were shining.

"I think he left because of us. Me and my sister. I think Aunt Jane and my mom used to blame each other so my sister and I wouldn't think it was us."

"That must have been terrible."

"I'm going to pack up his clothes and send them to a charity while my mom's out of town. Or maybe I'll set them on fire."

He partly suppressed a smile. "You think that's a good idea?"

"Don't worry, dude." Megan patted him on the shoulder. "I'll give you first pick of any good stuff. Green's your color. I know that."

"I don't want your dad's old clothes," he said. "And I'm not your dad. I'm not going to abandon you."

"You can't say that. You don't know what's going to happen in the future."

"You're right," he said, nodding solemnly. "All I can do is be completely honest and committed in the moment. That's all either of us can do."

"If I ever wanted you to come to a private therapy session with me, would you do that?"

"If that was something you wanted to do, I'd be happy to."

"Don't get too excited. I may have worked out all my problems already. I had some really weird dreams today, and…" She realized she was whistling through the hole in the front of her teeth. "Ma toof," she said.

Drew ducked his head and used his thumb to lift her upper lip. "Not again," he said. "What did I tell you about the pliers? You don't need an excuse to see me."

"Your office manager knocked it out. I banged into her in the hallway when I was running through your house like some sort of idiot to come see you." She pointed to the white lump on the bathroom's gleaming marble counter. "There's ma toof. Can you glue it back on?"

Drew examined the cap. "This isn't going back on. It's cracked. It wouldn't last one course, and then you'd swallow it, which is not something anyone wants." He tucked the cracked pieces into his shirt pocket. "We'll have to make you a new one."

She groaned. "This is going to cost me an arm and a leg, isn't it?"

"Just one kiss," he said.

"Just one?"

He closed the bathroom door. She gave him more than just one kiss.

He managed to eventually tear himself away from her embrace. His clothes were nearly as wet as hers.

"To be continued later," he said.

Drew opened the bathroom door. The sounds of music, laughter, and light conversation floated in.

Megan said, "Quite the event you have going on here, Dr. Morgan."

"It was going to be a small dinner for five or six, but Alan got carried away." He winced apologetically. "There's an ice sculpture."

"I've never been to anything with an ice sculpture," Megan said. She covered her jack-o'-lantern smile. "You don't want me to meet your friends looking like this. I can sneak out of here. Nobody needs to know, assuming Candy and Alan can keep their mouths shut. We can do this some other time, after you've fixed ma toof."

"Don't you dare leave," he said. "Alan will cry."

"He does look like a crier."

"It's the glasses," Drew said.

Megan shrugged. "I guess I can stay for a bit since I'm already here."

Drew led her out to the dining room where a dozen young, attractive, well-dressed people all stopped talking at once and looked up at them.

A new table setting had been squeezed in next to Drew's vacant chair.

Candy gave Megan a friendly wave from the distant end of the long table.

Drew said, "Everyone, this is my girlfriend, Megan Gardenia." He turned to her and asked, "Are you going by Megan now? Is that what you'd prefer?"

"That's who I am," she said to him. To the group, she said, "If that's too many syllables, you can call me Meg, but not Megs."

Alan asked, "What about Meggy, like Peggy?"

Megan went over to where Alan was seated, placed her hand on his shoulder, and said, "Happy birthday, Alan. It's so nice to meet you. Your brother's wrong about one thing. You don't look a day over... *forty*."

Everyone laughed, especially Alan.

Megan said to Alan, "You can call me Meggy if you want, but only for tonight, and only because it's your birthday."

He got up and hugged her. The Morgan boys were huggers apparently.

"I'm glad you made it after all," Alan said. "Thank you for the flowers. You're going to make a great addition to... my birthday party."

As Megan made her way around the long table, she got the feeling Alan had been about to welcome her to the family. Maybe it had just been her imagination, but she liked the new feeling of interpreting people's subtle gestures in a positive way.

She took her seat, next to Drew.

The next course was served, and the party resumed.

Alan was the center of attention, which Megan liked, because it gave her and Drew the chance to hold hands and give each other looks of flirtation and longing all through dinner.

The Morgan boys' friends were a nice mix of work colleagues and old friends from school. None of the rugby guys were there. The friends who were there weren't stuffy at all, and everyone teased Alan about the ice sculpture, which was a swan.

Throughout the evening, Alan kept bringing up the Morgans' mother and giving Drew meaningful glances.

Every time he did, Drew squeezed Megan's hand.

Chapter 36

Tuesday

Megan Gardenia walked into the group therapy session. The real one, not the dream one where Feather was twenty feet tall and nursing half a dozen babies. In real life, Feather was hiding her baby bump under a gray cloak.

The session hadn't started yet, so Megan said to Feather, "Full disclosure. I am dating Drew Morgan."

"I thought I detected a spring in your step."

"We are back on, and it's been rock solid for the last three days, so *that's* happening."

"Three days is a start," Feather said.

"Is it cool that I'm here?"

Feather said, "That depends. Are you going to let me run the group?"

"Sorry about last week," Megan said. "Things got out of control, and I got carried away. Do you despise me now for trying to take over?"

"Not at all. I have a lot of respect for what you did."

"I was pretty good at solving people's problems," Megan said. "And can you believe I have zero training whatsoever?"

"It's… hard to believe some of the things I've seen you do."

"And that's my secret sauce," Megan said. "It's what keeps the group from falling asleep."

"That must be it." Feather opened her arms. "May I hug you?"

"Sure." Megan hugged the group's coach. She noticed the baby bump was where it should be and didn't feel like it had multiple perfect babies inside.

Feather patted Megan lightly on the back and spoke softly near her ear. "Actually, I think last week was a success. I wasn't feeling up to speed, but we made some real progress, thanks to you."

"Is everything okay in your baby oven?"

"Everything's perfect. I'll make the announcement soon."

They came out of the hug. Megan said, "I know I did good work last week, but the ends didn't justify the means. I know I was out of line."

"Sometimes the line can be blurry," Feather said. "Life isn't black and white."

"I'm starting to get that," Megan said.

"Moving forward, I'm going to encourage the group's members to be more proactive in their lives. But we can't push people too far, too fast."

"Not these people," Megan said with a hand wave. "As for me, I want you to push me as hard as you can. I can take it."

Feather nodded slowly, her light, pretty eyes twinkling. "Drew has been good for you," she said. "He's done a lot in three days."

"He's a great guy. You know what? He'd be good for anyone. Literally, any girl. Sometimes I feel like I'm hogging him all to myself, and it's not fair."

"That's a good feeling to have, and don't ever doubt that you deserve it. We don't have to be perfect to deserve love."

"That's funny. My aunt said that to me in a dream."

"It's something I always say, Megan. I say it at least once, every meeting."

Megan gave the blonde her side-eye. "Are you sure about that? I'm pretty sure my subconscious came up with it all by itself."

Feather blinked slowly. "Perhaps your subconscious did," she said softly. "I'm going to borrow it from now on, if you don't mind."

"Be my guest. It's your group." Megan picked up the enormous tray of baked goods she had set on the table next to the sign-in book and took it over to the snack table.

Carla was there, pouring a cup of coffee. "Hi, Meenie," she said.

"I'm going by Megan now. I'll still answer to the other name, and I won't be offended if you call me that, but it's not me anymore."

"I understand." Carla put six sugar cubes in her coffee.

"That's too much sugar," Megan said. "Your dentist would not approve."

"It's how I like it," Carla said. "It's what I'm used to."

"Just because we're used to something doesn't mean it's good for us." Megan glanced up and caught the look Feather was directing at her. Megan said to Carla, "But that's just my opinion, and opinions are like butts. Everyone's got one."

"That's true," Carla said.

Megan looked into Carla's eyes and said, "I'm really sorry you lost Max. He must have been a spectacular dog. I wish I'd gotten to know him."

Carla took Megan's hand and squeezed it. "That's very sweet of you. You're a sweet girl."

"You don't have to get another dog if you don't want to," Megan said. "But I think another dog would be happy to have you."

Carla nodded then went to sit in the circle.

Jim came by for coffee next.

Megan said, "Jim, I'm sorry I said those things about your wife."

He avoided eye contact. "We're not supposed to talk about that stuff during the pleasantries."

"I'm going to apologize to you again in front of everyone too. I just wanted you to know that I mean it, Jim. I really do."

"Okay," he said. "Fair enough." He gave her a wary look as he edged away. "We'll see," he said.

When the librarian came by for her coffee, Megan said, "Francine, right? That's your name?"

"Yes," the woman said.

"I'm sorry I always think of you as the librarian, and that I keep forgetting your name."

"You do?" She looked hurt.

"Francine, you let me know if Jim does anything you don't like. I'll have a word with him, personally." She smacked her fist into her open palm.

"Sure," Francine the Librarian said. "Maybe we can get a cup of tea some time when our boys are out fishing."

"I'd like that," Megan said.

There was a line forming behind Francine.

Ryan was next and then Abbie and then some of the others.

One by one, Megan apologized to each one of them and tried to make amends. The people in line heard what was being said and figured out what was going on. For a few of them, this wasn't their only help group. When Megan had a difficult time remembering what she might have done to offend them, they gave her a list.

Despite the potential for awkwardness, it wasn't confrontational or upsetting for anyone. There were plenty of laughs and hugs.

Then Feather clapped her hands to get everyone's attention, and they gathered in their circle to start the session.

Ryan was wearing a new scarf.

Megan kept her opinions to herself as much as she could.

Chapter 37

Dr. Drew Morgan kept fidgeting with something in his pocket.

Megan was over at the Morgan brothers' house, having a casual dinner with Drew and his brother, Alan. It was casual in the sense that there were only three courses and no ice sculpture.

When Alan left the room to get dessert, Megan said, "If you don't give me whatever's in your pocket, I'm going to reach in there and grab it myself."

He got a devilish grin and threw his hands in the air. "Help yourself!"

She reached in and found a ring. Not an engagement ring but a ring with a large stone in the middle. A cheap-looking stone.

Megan frowned. "Is this plastic?"

"It's a mood ring," he said. "I bought it at a carnival when I was a kid. I wore it to school once because I thought it was cool. I got my first black eye that day."

"You got bullied?"

"Not exactly. The guy who punched me once got two right back."

She handed the ring back. "You can wear it now, if you want. You're an adult. Nobody's going to beat you up." She made a fist and punched her palm. "Not if they don't want me to tag in and finish the match."

He put the ring back in his pocket. "Never mind," he said.

She put her hand in his pocket and grabbed the ring back. "Don't tell me to never mind. Why do you have this? Were you going to give it to me?"

"I thought it would be funny," he said. "You're reading all those books Feather recommended, and you're doing that thing where you name your emotions. I thought it would be funny if you had a mood ring to help you with that."

She tried on the ring. The only finger it fit was her ring finger, so she left it there. "I like it," she said. "It's not very funny, though. It's actually kind of…" She was at a loss for words. It had been happening a lot lately. Coming up with words to describe feelings was much harder than being crass or sarcastic.

"Romantic," Drew said.

"Yeah. I guess you're right. It's romantic." She leaned over and gave him a kiss on the cheek.

"Plus, now I know your ring size," he said.

They both looked down at her hand.

She looked away.

"For the future," he said. "Relax. I don't mean right now."

She looked at the ring again. It was changing colors.

"It's working," she said.

"It's a heat-sensitive compound," he said. "It doesn't really tell you someone's mood, just how warm their fingers are."

"But finger temperature means a lot," she said. "I've been reading about the nervous system, and how everything works together in all these different feedback loops. When someone's stressed, their hands get cold. Or when their hands get cold for some other reason, they might *feel* stressed and make up a story about why they feel that way. People make up a lot of stories to explain how they feel because it's so confusing to not know, and sometimes we'd rather think it's because of something bad than not know at all."

He looked down at the ring, which was still changing colors. "I had no idea."

"I'll have to come into your clinic and give you some tips for putting your patients more at ease."

"You can't do that," he said. "It would really cut down on the screaming, which I have grown to love." He gave her his mad scientist cackle.

"You are so weird." She kissed him again.

Alan returned with the dessert, which was enormous.

Drew chided him. "That's too much for three people."

"One does not make a *small* Baked Alaska," Alan said. "Everyone knows that. It's the sort of thing that doesn't scale well."

Alan looked at Megan's hand. "Is that your ring, Drew? I remember that thing."

Drew said, "It sure is. I'm using it to save a spot on Megan's finger for when I get her something better."

"Good idea," Alan said. "I like the way you think." He looked down at the enormous dessert, which was a meringue-coated ice cream cake that had been in a blazing hot oven briefly, so it was toasty and brown on the outside and cold on the inside. "Who wants a corner piece?"

"It's a circle," Drew said. "There are either no corners or infinite corners."

"Exactly," Alan said. "Everybody likes the corner piece with all the fun toppings because it's the best piece."

Drew reached over and squeezed Megan's knee. "It really is the best piece," he said.

Megan looked at her mood ring. It kept getting brighter and brighter.

If you enjoyed this novel, you'll love Angie Pepper's other books set on Baker Street, featuring more great romantic comedy plus guest appearances by your favorite characters!

For a full list of titles, visit the author's website at **www.angelapepper.com**

Thanks for reading!